HOMETOWN HEARTS

Baby's First Homecoming

New York Times Bestselling Author

CATHY McDAVID

HARLEQUIN® HOMETOWN HEARTS

Recycling programs
for this product may
not exist in your area.

ISBN-13: 978-0-373-21452-5

Baby's First Homecoming

Copyright © 2012 by Cathy McDavid

Printed in U.S.A.

HARLEQUIN®
™ www.Harlequin.com

HOMETOWN HEARTS

SHIPMENT 1

Stranger in Town by Brenda Novak
Baby's First Homecoming by Cathy McDavid
Her Surprise Hero by Abby Gaines
A Mother's Homecoming by Tanya Michaels
A Firefighter in the Family by Trish Milburn
Tempted by a Texan by Mindy Neff

SHIPMENT 2

It Takes a Family by Victoria Pade
The Sheriff of Heartbreak County by Kathleen Creighton
A Hometown Boy by Janice Kay Johnson
The Renegade Cowboy Returns by Tina Leonard
Unexpected Bride by Lisa Childs
Accidental Hero by Loralee Lillibridge

SHIPMENT 3

An Unlikely Mommy by Tanya Michaels
Single Dad Sheriff by Lisa Childs
In Protective Custody by Beth Cornelison
Cowboy to the Rescue by Trish Milburn
The Ranch She Left Behind by Kathleen O'Brien
Most Wanted Woman by Maggie Price
A Weaver Wedding by Allison Leigh

SHIPMENT 4

A Better Man by Emilie Rose
Daddy Protector by Jacqueline Diamond
The Road to Bayou Bridge by Liz Talley
Fully Engaged by Catherine Mann
The Cowboy's Secret Son by Trish Milburn
A Husband's Watch by Karen Templeton

Since 2006, *New York Times* bestselling author
Cathy McDavid has been happily penning contemporary
Westerns for Harlequin. Every day, she gets to write
about handsome cowboys riding the range or busting
a bronc. It's a tough job, but she's willing to make the
sacrifice. Cathy shares her Arizona home with her own
real-life sweetheart and a trio of odd pets. Her grown
twins have left to embark on lives of their own, and she
couldn't be prouder of their accomplishments.

To my son Clay. You were without a doubt the cutest, most charming little boy there ever was. One day I looked away for just a minute, and you grew up into a fine, talented, handsome young man. I am so very proud of you and all your accomplishments.

Love you always, Mom.

Chapter One

The Powell family home, more than a century old, had been transformed. Sierra Powell stood beside the open door of her Toyota SUV, assessing every change, comparing them to how she'd last seen the house, in shocking disrepair after ten years of chronic neglect.

Trees were trimmed, the yard's abundant desert flora and fauna manicured to tidy perfection. A fresh coat of dune-colored paint on the house's exterior gleamed to eye-squinting intensity in the midafternoon sun. Terra-cotta bricks lined the walkways to the front courtyard and back patio, resembling spectators at a parade.

The refurbishings pleased Sierra. It had taken a long time for her family to rebound from the emotional and financial ruin left in the wake of her mother's illness and death. These improvements to the house, she knew, mirrored the ones in her father and two brothers.

She envied them. The Powell men were healed and happy and well on the way to creating wonderful, exciting new lives for themselves while she had never been so terrified of the future or felt so alone.

What if her family rejected her? They certainly had good cause—she'd practically shunned them for almost two years. Now she'd returned, not just for her brothers' double wedding but to ask for her family's help, their love, their support, and, if they could see fit to give it, their forgiveness.

It wouldn't be easy. Sierra had made a lot of mistakes.

She stared at the back patio, working up the courage to head inside where her family and future sisters-in-law waited. Everyone was expecting her, possibly intending to confront her. There would be questions, especially when they saw the unexpected "guest" Sierra had brought with her and heard her request to— temporarily, she assured herself—move home.

By some miracle she'd been able to stand outside this long without being noticed. Maybe no one was home. She immediately dismissed that idea. Someone would be here to greet her. Her father at least, who'd insisted she come home for her brothers' double wedding.

Her brothers, Gavin and Ethan, could be elsewhere on the ranch—leading trail rides, teaching riding classes or otherwise making themselves scarce so she and her father could have a few minutes alone. She had hurt him the worst and owed him the biggest apology. It was he who had the power to grant or deny her request to stay.

Sierra might have been lost in thought indefinitely if not for a noise coming from inside her car. She opened the rear driver's-side door and stuck her head inside.

"Hey, handsome. You awake? How was your nap?"

Her son waved his pudgy fists and broke into a delighted grin that displayed six new teeth. His hazel eyes, the image of his father's, beamed at her as he babbled incoherently.

Her heart promptly broke open and spilled a torrent of love as it did every time he smiled or gurgled or nuzzled into her neck and sighed with baby contentment.

"Thank God I have you back," she murmured for the thousandth time, a catch in her voice, the wound within her still raw.

She didn't know what she'd done to deserve this reprieve. This gift. This chance to right past wrongs. But she was bound and determined to turn her life around and make the best one possible for her and her son. If she needed to get on her hands and knees and beg her family, she would. He was that important to her.

"Let's clean you up a bit before we meet the folks." Using a cotton cloth, she wiped the smudges of dirt from his face and hands. "There. All better."

He kicked his feet, which were clad in white socks and brand-new red sneakers she'd recently purchased. In fact, she'd recently purchased all his clothes, the car seat, a portable crib and every necessity a child his age needed.

She reached onto the seat beside him and retrieved his favorite toy from where it had fallen. He grabbed the plastic pony and waved it in the air as if to say, Where have you been? I was looking for you, and stuffed the pony's entire head in his mouth.

With trembling fingers, Sierra unbuckled

the car-seat straps. The distraction of caring for her son had worn off. She was once again dreading the prospect of facing her family.

They love you, she told herself. *They will love Jamie, too.*

But was it enough to make up for the last two years of shameful avoidance?

Drawing a deep breath, she hefted Jamie into her arms. When he was securely balanced on her hip and the diaper bag was slung over her shoulder, she picked her way slowly up the brick-lined walk to the back patio.

The kitchen door loomed ahead, the outline wavering as if she were seeing it though a very long tunnel. Her flats made scuffing sounds on the dirt and then clip-clopped across the Saltillo tiles, each beat matching her pounding heart.

Thank goodness she didn't have to worry about Jamie's father being anywhere near Mustang Valley. The last she'd heard, which was soon after their too-brief affair ended, he was married and living in Austin, Texas. Sierra had taken a risk returning to Arizona, but a small one so long as he stayed far, far away.

And she needed that distance, for her sake more than their son's. His betrayal—she couldn't think of it any other way—had shattered her. Granted, she'd been naive. That in no way made it acceptable for him to take advantage of her.

She reached the kitchen door and found it slightly ajar. Odd.

Knocking, she called, "Hello! Dad?" When there was no answer, she knocked again.

The door drifted open a few more inches. Sierra nudged it the rest of the way and stepped tentatively inside.

"Hello. Anybody home?"

The only answer she received was the soft humming of the refrigerator and the whirr of the slowly twirling ceiling fan over the kitchen table.

She frowned. This was more than strange. Her family knew she was coming. Heck, she'd called her father not an hour ago letting him know her anticipated arrival time.

She ventured farther in. It was then she noticed a large sheet cake in the center of the counter. Inching closer, she read the message scrawled with blue icing.

Welcome Home, Sissy. Her family's pet name for her.

Was it possible they weren't angry with her after all?

A dam broke, and the relief washing over her was so intense it stole every ounce of strength from her knees. She reached for the counter to steady herself before the combined weight of Jamie and the diaper bag dragged her to the floor.

"Surprise!" The resounding chorus of voices erupted from nowhere, echoing loudly off the walls. People, so many of them, converged on her from around corners and down the hall.

No, no!

Sierra's entire body jerked in response, out of alarm and fear. This wasn't how it was supposed to happen.

"You're here, honey!"

"Hey, Sissy."

"We've missed you!"

Jamie screwed up his mouth and started to wail. Holding on to her, he hid his beet-red face in her sweater. His beloved toy pony dropped to the floor, along with the diaper bag.

The room went instantly silent, like a TV when the mute button was pressed. Even Jamie stopped crying and turned teary eyes to the gathering of people gawking at him.

A young girl of about six or seven whom Sierra didn't recognize broke the silence with an excited, "You have a baby! Can I hold him?" She scrambled over to Sierra, her angelic face alight. "I'm Isa, your niece. Or I'm going to be your niece when my mama marries your brother."

"Hello, Isa." Sierra had trouble speaking and cleared her throat. "I've heard a lot about you."

Actually, Sierra had heard only a smattering about her future stepniece. She might have heard more if she'd answered her family's phone calls or read their emails.

Glancing around the kitchen, she took in the puzzled and shocked expressions on everyone's faces. Except for Isa, they kept their distance, as if waiting for someone else to break the ice.

What had she expected? She'd brought a fourteen-month-old child home with her, and had given them no warning.

Her oldest brother, Gavin, studied her with his usual seriousness. As a girl, she had been intimidated by that look. Living on her own since she was seventeen apparently made no difference.

Ethan, younger than Gavin by two years, nodded encouragingly at her. He'd always been there for her—except for when their mother had died almost a decade ago, and he'd run off to join the marines.

Everyone else was a blur. Some she recognized, like Ethan's fiancée, Caitlin. Others, she didn't.

"I like babies." Isa reached up to tickle Jamie under his chin.

He flailed and turned his head away from her. Isa pouted.

"He's a little shy," Sierra explained.

"Well, well." Her father finally came forward, breaking the trance that had fallen over everyone. The reserved smile he presented reassured Sierra not in the least. "Why don't you introduce us to this young man."

"Dad," Sierra said shakily, "this is Jamie. My…my son." Her hand instinctively cradled the side of the baby's head as if to shield him.

Her father's reserved smile dissolved into one that warmed her through and through. "I have a grandson. Oh, Sierra." He opened his arms.

She went to him, let him hug her and Jamie and, temporarily, set right a world that had been completely out of control for almost two years.

"I'm so sorry," she murmured into his shirt-front.

"Don't be. Everything's going to be fine. You'll see."

She wanted to believe him, and dared to let herself.

Jamie squirmed and started to cry.

Sierra drew back, reluctant to leave the comfort of her father's embrace. "He's hungry. I'd better fix him something to eat."

"Can I hold him while you do?" her father asked.

"He doesn't like—" She'd started to say *strangers*. Not wanting to hurt her father's feelings, she changed it to "New people."

He held open his arms. Jamie stared at them, a dubious frown knitting his otherwise perfectly smooth brow. When his grandfather clapped his hands and held them open again, Jamie twisted and reached for Sierra.

Her father's smile fell.

"He'll get used to you in a day or two," she reassured him, though, in truth, she didn't know what to expect. She and Jamie were still getting to know each other.

Her brothers came over next. Ethan's hug was enthusiastic. Gavin's less so. He loved her, but he was also angry at her for the pain she'd caused them and slower to let go of hard feelings.

"I'm so happy for you both," she said. "I can't wait for the wedding."

That seemed to ease the tension. More introductions were made. Sierra greeted Caitlin warmly, having known Ethan's fiancée since grade school. Sage, Gavin's fiancée, impressed Sierra with her genuineness.

"Your son is beautiful." Sage patted Jamie's leg.

He jerked his leg out of her reach.

Sierra smiled apologetically. "He's hungry and a little cranky."

While she warmed a jar of baby vegetable stew in the microwave, Jamie, still sitting on her hip, polished off a bottle of apple juice. Everyone began talking again, thank goodness.

After a while, Gavin's daughter, Cassie, came over. "I'm a good babysitter if you ever need one."

"Thanks." Sierra patted the girl's shoulder. "I'll keep that in mind."

She hadn't met Cassie before. The twelve-year-old had only come to live at the ranch last summer. Sierra noticed the affectionate glances Gavin sent his daughter from across the room. Maybe one day she'd have the same loving relationship with Jamie.

"It's so nice to have another baby in the family," Caitlin said, joining Sierra at the table where she fed Jamie.

"Another baby?"

"Sage is four months along, and I'm two."

"You're both pregnant!"

Sage dropped into the remaining empty chair. "Yes, so I guess it's a good thing the wedding's soon! I wouldn't fit into my dress otherwise."

"Congratulations." Sierra observed the joy in their faces and felt a pang of regret. Her face had been a mask of sorrow all during her pregnancy.

"Is Jamie's father in San Francisco?" Caitlin asked.

Sierra tensed. She'd prepared herself for this question on the long drive. "He's not part of mine or Jamie's lives. I'm raising him alone."

She couldn't tell her family the truth. If they ever found out Jamie's father was the son of the man who'd stolen their land and sold it to an investor, they'd disown Sierra and toss her and Jamie out on their rear ends.

Near the end of the meal, Sierra excused herself and went to the hall bathroom to clean up Jamie and change him.

On her way back, she was stopped outside the kitchen by a chorus of hearty welcomes and the sound of a voice that instantly ignited wave after wave of panic.

Clay Duvall.

Impossible! This couldn't be happening.

He was in Texas. And even if he wasn't, her family hated him. He wouldn't be allowed on the property, much less to set foot in the house.

"Sissy, come see who's here," her brother Ethan called to her.

She trembled so violently, she nearly dropped Jamie. He made it worse by wriggling.

"Hey." Ethan came around the corner. "Is something wrong?"

"What's he doing here?" she hissed.

"Clay? He came to see you."

"Why?"

"He's a friend."

"No, he isn't. His dad cheated us. You hate him. We all do."

"Not anymore."

"Since when?" she squeaked.

"Since we captured the wild mustang last fall. It's a long story, I'll tell you after the party." Ethan hooked her by the elbow and gave a tug.

She refused to budge.

"Come on. You haven't seen Clay since before Mom died."

Not true.

Ethan all but dragged her and Jamie into the kitchen where she stumbled into her chair, praying for invisibility. Her family and Clay were friends again? How could that be? In every scenario she'd devised, he'd been a thousand miles away.

He strode farther into the kitchen.

Please, please, don't come over here, she silently prayed.

Of course, he did, and she steeled herself.

"Hi, Sierra." His smile was friendly, his voice deep and honeyed like she remembered.

She looked up at him—how could she not?—and stared into the face of her baby's father. Her heart, open with love for her son and the recent reconciliation with her family, promptly closed tight.

She had a baby.

Clay's stomach clenched as if someone had sucker-punched him with the business end of a baseball bat.

From the moment he'd learned Sierra was returning to Mustang Valley, he'd imagined them picking up where they'd left off. She'd generously overlook his incredible lack of judgment and brief, disastrous marriage, and they'd fall into each other's arms.

Only her arms were full of a bouncing baby boy. There went the happy-you're-home kiss he'd been counting on.

Instead, he squeezed her upper arm. "Good to see you again."

She muttered something about how nice it was to see him, too.

The boy's head tipped back, and his inquisitive gaze fixed on Clay's face. There was something about his eyes that struck a familiar chord, though Clay couldn't quite identify why.

Maybe he was wrong, and the kid wasn't hers. She could be a nanny or something.

"Who's this?" he asked.

"My, um, my…" She glanced down at the baby, held him closer. "My son."

Clay swallowed. So much for his nanny theory.

Which meant she'd been with a man. A man besides him. Jealousy sliced through him. Not that he had any claim on her. He'd forfeited it the second he'd stupidly left Sierra in order to reunite with Jessica, his then ex-fiancée and later wife.

In hindsight, hurting Sierra had been inevitable.

If Gavin and Ethan knew what he'd done to their little sister, he'd lose a lot more than their friendship. An arm. The use of his legs. And that was just for starters.

"What's his name?" Clay asked.

The baby babbled as if answering. He really was an appealing tyke. Clay felt an unfamiliar, but not unpleasant, tug inside his chest. He'd always liked kids despite having little experience with them and would be a father today if things had gone differently.

His loss still pained him.

Probably the reason he felt drawn to Sierra's boy.

She said nothing, acting as though she hadn't heard him. Loading a spoon with some vile-looking mush out of a jar, she tried to feed it to the baby. Wisely, the kid shook his head and grimaced. The stuff did look awful.

"No name, buddy?"

"It's Jamie," Isa piped up. She and Cassie had been standing behind Sierra and trying to distract the baby with funny faces. "Isn't that a cool name?"

"Yeah," Clay agreed, receiving yet another invisible punch to the stomach. "Cool."

His grandfather's name had been Jamie, short for Jamieson. Did Sierra know?

Yes, he'd told her all about his summers spent in Montana and about returning for his grandfather's funeral.

Coincidence?

It had to be.

"Nice to meet you, Jamie," Clay said and leaned down, extending his index finger.

The baby broke into a wide, rather comical grin and grabbed Clay's finger, holding it as if he were shaking hands.

"He likes you," Cassie blurted.

"The feeling's mutual." The tug inside Clay's chest grew stronger, and he grinned back at the baby. Turning his head, he discovered Sierra's face mere inches from him. "Cute baby."

She stared back at him, her brown eyes wide with terror.

His grin dissolved, and he involuntarily straightened. The moment he did, she practically leapt out of her chair.

"I'd better clean this up." Grabbing the jar of baby food and empty bottle with her free hand, she cut past Isa and made a hasty bee-line for the sink, Jamie riding on her hip.

What exactly had happened?

He would have understood anger. He'd treated her badly after all. But fear? No. Something else was definitely amiss.

Clay's glance cut to Sage and Caitlin still sitting at the table. Their expressions reflected a confusion similar to the one he was experiencing.

The celebration continued with cake and punch. Wayne Powell, Sierra's father, acted as host. The group of men, which included a few family friends and two of the Powells' longtime ranch hands, wandered to the living room. The women, girls and Wayne remained in the kitchen, hovering around Sierra and Jamie.

Clay stayed, too, using a conversation with Wayne as his excuse. While the older man talked, Clay kept one ear tuned to the discussion going on between the women.

Sierra had set Jamie on the floor, and he was toddling about by her feet. Isa knelt in front of him, making a toy pony that looked as if it had been mauled gallop in the air.

"How old is he?" Caitlin asked Sierra.

Sierra hesitated, thinned her lips and twirled

a strand of glossy brunette hair around her finger. "About a year."

Clay knew that look and habit, having seen it a hundred times before. He'd spent almost as much time at Powell Ranch as he had his own family's while growing up. Sierra was the pesky, always-in-the-way little sister. While she didn't lie, exactly, she'd occasionally exaggerated, and the hair-twirling was a dead giveaway.

So, what was she exaggerating about this time?

"He's walking well for a year," Sage commented.

"Did he have his birthday already?" Cassie asked. "Maybe we can have a party for him."

Sierra thinned her lips again and twirled her hair even faster. "He already had a party."

Wayne said something to Sierra about her and Jamie staying in Ethan's old room, that her room had been given over to the girls.

Clay listened and watched.

Jamie fascinated him. He picked at the laces of Isa's sneakers with amazing determination and quickly had them untied. Clay admired that quality, having plenty of it himself. He'd inherited it from his father and grandfather Jamie.

Suddenly, the air was too thick to breathe and the room stifling hot.

Clay mentally calculated how long since he and Sierra had last seen each other. Last slept together. Not quite two years. She had mentioned Jamie was about a year. But if he was older, say thirteen or fourteen months...

She'd lied, and not just about Jamie's age.

"Sierra." The volume of Clay's voice surprised not only himself but everyone else in the room. He didn't care. "We need to talk."

The fear he'd seen in her face earlier returned tenfold, only now he knew the cause.

When she didn't move, he started toward her. "Right this minute."

"I—I—" She bent and picked up Jamie, who was not happy about being separated from Isa and started to wail. "I really should unload the car."

"I'll help you."

"What's going on?" Wayne moved to stand in front of Clay.

"This is between me and Sierra."

Wayne might be pushing sixty but he presented a formidable obstacle when protecting his daughter. "Whatever you have to say to her, you can say to me."

"Is that what you want?" Clay's gaze locked with Sierra's.

"No." Her answer was hardly more than a whisper.

He went to the kitchen door, opened it and waited for her to join him.

"Sierra, you don't have to go with him." Wayne laid a protective hand on her arm.

She squared her shoulders. "It's okay, Dad."

She was brave, he'd give her that much.

"No, it's not," Wayne said. "I don't like him ordering you around." The glare Wayne shot Clay reminded him it hadn't been *that* long since he'd reconciled with the Powells.

He didn't care. He'd lost one child already, he wasn't about to lose a second.

"You harm one hair on her head—"

Clay cut off Wayne before he could finish. "I won't. I swear."

Wayne reluctantly backed off, his narrowed gaze informing Clay they weren't done by a long shot.

When Sierra reached the door, he held out his arms to Jamie. "Let me take him."

"No!" She curled her body away from Clay. "He doesn't like strangers."

Jamie made a liar of his mother by extending his arms to Clay. She held fast but lost her grip when Jamie squirmed and wriggled sideways.

Clay caught the boy easily and balanced him on his hip as he'd seen Sierra do.

"Give him back," she demanded.

"I will, after you and I talk."

Sierra went outside with Clay. Whatever she felt, she did a good job of keeping it to herself.

Clay was ready to explode.

They'd no sooner stepped off the back patio when he stopped and reeled on her.

"How dare you keep my son from me!"

Chapter Two

"Let me explain," Sierra insisted, jogging to match Clay's long strides.

"You lied to me."

He was right. She'd done everything in her power to hide Jamie's existence from him. Worse, if there was any way she could go back in time to an hour ago, she'd drive past her family's ranch and keep driving until she found someplace safe.

"Give Jamie to me, I can—"

"He's fine."

And he was fine, if his silly grin and happy babbling was any indication. Damn Clay.

She wanted to cry out, tackle Clay and

wrestle Jamie away from him. It would be fruitless, of course. Clay was easily six-two and strong as a linebacker. What if he took off with Jamie? Made a mad dash to his truck? She might never get her son back.

"Please, Clay." She strived to maintain a reasonable tone. "If we could just talk."

"We'll talk, all right. But not here. I don't want your family interfering."

Her family! Oh, God, what must they be thinking? They'd barely begun to accept she had a child and now this. Surely her father was putting two and two together. They might have made their peace with Clay, but he'd still been their hated enemy when he and Sierra had their affair.

Clay crossed the open area and headed toward the stables, her son still clutched in his arms.

Her son.

Yes, his son, too. That, however, was a technicality. Clay hadn't wanted her when given the chance, had chosen to marry his off-again, on-again fiancée instead. As far as Sierra was concerned, he'd forfeited any and all say regarding Jamie.

It was an opinion Clay didn't seem to share.

"Wait!" Sierra hurried to catch up. "I'll carry Jamie. He doesn't like strangers."

"I'm no stranger." Clay didn't take his eyes off the ground in front of him. "I'm his father."

Anger bloomed inside her. "Clay, I said wait!"

He slowed, then, to her relief, came to a halt. She drew up beside him, weak-kneed from exertion as much as emotional overload.

Jamie hung on to Clay's neck and giggled.

Maybe he really did like other people, and she was the one with the phobia.

It was possible.

No one other than the pediatrician during their visit to his office last Monday had been allowed to hold Jamie besides Sierra. She didn't count the months between his birth and three weeks ago when he'd been returned to her. The Stevensons, the ones who'd cared for him, didn't matter. Didn't exist. Not after rejecting her child.

"Where are you taking us?" She captured Jamie's flailing foot in her hand and cupped the ankle, desperately needing the contact. He had been no more than an arm's length away from her since the minute she'd got him back.

"Ethan's apartment."

Sierra remembered now. Her brother had converted the old bunkhouse into an apartment after Sage and Isa moved into the main house.

"We can be alone there and lock the door."

"Lock the door?" She shook her head. "Aren't you being a little extreme?"

"No, considering the cavalry's almost here."

Sierra looked behind her. Her dad and brothers were indeed coming after them. The three sweetest, most important and ridiculously overprotective men in the world were going to rescue her. She had half a mind to let them. Then, she remembered Clay's hardheadedness. He wouldn't give up Jamie without a fight.

"Let me talk to them."

"I'll meet you in the apartment."

Inside? Out of her sight?

"No!" The mere thought of being away from her baby paralyzed her.

The muscles in Clay's jaw were clenching with anger or impatience or frustration, she didn't know which. "I won't take off with him."

She exhaled slowly. How to explain her crippling separation anxiety? She barely understood it herself.

"I'll go with you to Ethan's apartment.

Anywhere you want. Just stay where I can see Jamie until I'm done talking to the family. Please."

"Fine, I'll wait for you on the porch."

Sierra mentally measured the distance. Thirty yards, give or take. It felt more like ten miles.

"You have about three seconds to decide."

Or what? He would go back on his word and run off with Jamie? Her temples throbbed. This day, her entire life, was unraveling at lightning speed.

"Okay."

As soon as Clay walked away, Sierra regretted her decision. He would be alone with her son. Never once had she imagined Clay would walk into her family's house and steal Jamie from her like an eagle snatching prey.

With one eye trained on Clay and Jamie, she braced herself for the confrontation with her father and brothers.

"Are you all right?" Wayne Powell demanded the instant he reached her. "What's going on?"

Gavin zoomed past without so much as a glance in her direction.

"Come back!" she called. When he ignored

her, she hollered, "Gavin, don't make this worse than it already is."

That did the trick. Fists clenched at his sides, he returned, each step an obvious effort.

Sierra closed her eyes and sighed. Where to begin?

"Is he Jamie's father?"

She nodded.

"Son of a bitch," Gavin grumbled. "I'll kill him."

"Don't overreact. He didn't—" Sierra squeezed her eyes shut. "It was mutual. I knew what I was doing."

"If you loved him, why didn't you tell us?" Ethan asked.

How had he guessed? "You despised Clay at the time. Can you imagine your reaction?"

"Damn straight I can," Gavin agreed.

"Is that why you stayed away so long?" her father asked.

"Dad, I didn't mean to hurt you. I was confused. I came home for the wedding because I thought Clay was in Texas."

"He moved back a year or so ago. After his divorce."

"He's divorced?" She swayed slightly. "I didn't know."

Not that it made any difference.

Or did it?

No difference at all, she assured herself. There was nothing between her and Clay, now or ever again.

Except for Jamie.

"If you thought he was in Texas, why didn't you come home sooner?" her father asked, his eyes filled with sadness.

Guilt burned a brand-new hole in Sierra, bigger than all the other ones combined.

"It's complicated. And I'll tell you as soon as I finish with Clay."

He'd begun pacing on the porch. From this distance, Sierra couldn't tell if it was because he'd become restless or Jamie had or perhaps a combination of both. Neither man nor child possessed much patience, and both were prone to impulsiveness. They were also both charming to distraction when it suited them.

"You going to be okay?" Ethan squeezed her upper arm.

"With Clay? Of course. He's mad right at the moment, but he won't do anything drastic."

"I wasn't referring to Clay."

"Thank you for caring." She smiled tenderly at all three men. "I can't tell you how much I regret the way I treated you the last two years."

"Don't worry, honey." Her father gathered her into a hug and patted her head, much as he'd done when she was a little girl. "Everything will work out."

She wished she shared his optimism.

"We'll be right here if you need us." Gavin stared menacingly at Clay.

"Watch him for me, will you?" Sierra asked Ethan. "I don't want him going all big-brother on me."

"Don't be so hard on Gavin," her father said. "It's going to take us a while to get used to all this."

To say the least.

The walk to the apartment took forever and yet was over in an instant. Sierra climbed the three porch steps with leaden feet and a racing heart.

Clay stood by the door with one hand on the knob, his expression guarded and grave.

Her son's, on the other hand, lit up at the sight of her, and he babbled excitedly, just as he had three weeks ago when he'd seen her for the first time since the day he was born.

Giving Jamie up for adoption was the hardest thing she'd ever done.

Facing Clay, telling him about it, was coming in a very close second.

"He wants down." Sierra sat on the couch, assuming, hoping that Clay would sit there, too, and Jamie would crawl across the cushions to her.

Only Clay had chosen the chair, a hand-me-down that used to reside in the living room long before she'd left for college.

Jamie squirmed and wriggled and whined, pushing ruthlessly at Clay's chest in a bid for freedom. The resemblance between them, same hazel eyes and blond hair, same disarming smile, was striking enough for Sierra to realize she wouldn't have gotten away with lying about her child's father's identity for long.

"I won't take off with him," she repeated his earlier promise.

Clay released Jamie, reluctantly depositing him on the hardwood floor. He immediately scrambled over to Sierra, then abandoned her just as quickly to explore the cozy apartment. The two-person breakfast set fascinated him. He squeezed between a chair and the table legs, then plopped on the floor beneath the table, cooing with satisfaction.

Sierra hadn't visited the old bunkhouse in years. As with the main house, the transformation amazed her.

"Why didn't you tell me about Jamie?"

It was like Clay to ask the toughest question first.

She collected her thoughts before replying. "The simple answer is I found out you and Jessica were back together and getting married. Showing up at the wedding and announcing I was carrying your child didn't feel like the right thing to do."

"That's not reason enough. You denied me my son."

"Yes, I did." And she would do it again, given half the chance.

"Why?"

She wasn't going to admit she'd fallen in love during their two-week affair and that the announcement of his marriage so soon after it ended had crushed her. Clay would sense her vulnerability, and she wasn't about to give him any advantage.

"I denied myself my son, too," she said.

"I don't see how." He glowered at her as if she were a criminal when what she'd really been was a victim—of his callousness and the Stevensons' heartlessness.

"I didn't learn I was pregnant until after Dad told me you and Jessica had set a date."

"I'm sorry I didn't tell you myself." Clay's glower momentarily abated. "I owed you that much."

He had. And admitting it almost two years too late didn't diminish her anguish.

"I was never very regular," she continued without acknowledging his apology. "It wasn't until the flu bug I thought I'd caught didn't go away that I finally considered the possibility I was pregnant. You have to understand what a shock it was. We'd used protection."

"I do understand. But that's still no reason to keep Jamie a secret."

"I didn't tell my family, either, not that it matters."

"It does, actually. I was going to give Ethan and Gavin hell for not telling me."

"Today was the first I'd heard you and my brothers were friends again."

"More than friends. Gavin and I are partners in a mustang stud and breeding business, and Ethan works for me at the rodeo arena, breaking and training broncs."

"Wow!" Friends and business partners *and* coworkers. It was a lot for Sierra to absorb all at once.

"You'd have known we'd reconciled if you'd ever talked to your family."

"I deserved that." She may have, but it still stung.

"I didn't say it to be mean."

Hadn't he?

The glower had returned, raising her hackles.

"Regardless, at the time I found out I was pregnant, you and my family hated each other and had for years. Which is the reason we snuck around those two weeks."

"I wanted to tell them about us, if you remember."

"Right. Like I was supposed to say, 'Hey, Dad, I'm dating Clay, the son of the man who sold the land that was in our family for four generations.' They'd have disowned me."

"That's not true."

"They wouldn't have been happy. Dad despised your father."

"For the record, I never agreed with what he did to your family. We've hardly spoken in years."

"That's too bad."

"No, it isn't." Clay ground out the words as if they tasted foul.

Whatever had transpired between him and his father must have been quite ugly.

"He's family." Sierra was just now rediscovering how important family was, even when the parent was a soulless man like Bud Duvall.

"So is Jamie," Clay said. "My family."

They both looked at their son.

He'd grown bored with his pretend cave beneath the table and had crawled out. Before he could interest himself in an electrical outlet or a lamp cord, Sierra rose from the couch, located a ring of keys on the counter and gave them to him. Thrilled, he sat on the floor between the kitchen and living room and proceeded to investigate his new toy with avid concentration.

"I'd have taken care of you and Jamie," Clay said.

"You would have." His sense of duty was nothing if not strong. Unlike his father's. "Jessica, I was pretty sure, might have objected to you having a child with another woman."

He didn't answer, letting her know she was right.

"I refused to be responsible for ending your marriage before it even began."

"That was my decision to make. Not yours."

"Blame the hormones. I was confused and—" she decided to be honest with him "—hurt. I wasn't thinking entirely clearly."

She'd also been depressed. Deeply depressed. Enough that her obstetrician had become concerned and prescribed private counseling along with a support group. Sierra's health insurance didn't cover counseling, and she wasn't earning enough money to pay for it out of pocket. She did attend a support group. Three meetings. Talking with other single mothers in similar situations had only made her feel worse, not better.

Chronically sick, hormonal and at an all-time emotional low, she'd been an easy target for someone with a personal agenda. Like the Stevensons.

"I didn't intend to hurt you, Sierra. Those two weeks we had together were wonderful."

"Not wonderful enough, I guess." The wound he'd left her with ached anew.

"You were going back to San Francisco. My job was here. If I led you to believe we had a future—"

"You didn't."

Sierra had been the one to hope for the impossible. Clay and Jessica had dated for years. Six, no, seven. They were constantly breaking up, only to reconcile days or weeks later. Sierra had been a fool to think he wouldn't run back to Jessica the second she snapped her fingers.

"What made you decide to come home?" He'd gotten around at last to asking the second-toughest question.

She took her time, watching Jamie push the keys across the floor instead of answering Clay. It required all her willpower not to dash into the kitchen and grab Jamie. She didn't want to be here, didn't want to be having this conversation with Clay. What had made her think returning to Arizona was the solution?

"Sierra?"

"My brothers' wedding, of course. And I realized I needed help. Raising a child alone isn't easy."

"Are you home for good?"

"I…" Here was another chance to fib, but she couldn't. "I think so. I haven't discussed it with Dad yet."

"You weren't planning on telling me, were you? Not ever."

"I thought it best to get settled in first. Give my family time to adjust."

"Bullshit!"

"I told you, I thought you were in Texas."

"You could have found out easily enough if you'd bothered asking."

She shot to her feet. "You have no right to lecture me!"

"And you have no right to hide my son." He stood, too. "What was it? Revenge? Because I hurt you?"

"God, no!"

He snorted. "Right."

Jamie began to wail. One glance informed Sierra he was responding to her and Clay's escalating argument.

She went to him. Clay didn't object when she lifted Jamie into her arms. Patting his back, she murmured soothing phrases until he quieted. Before too long, he wanted down again.

When she released him, he toddled over to the cabinet under the sink where there was probably bleach, dish soap and a multitude of potentially dangerous cleaning products. Sierra opened an overhead cupboard and found some plastic cups and mugs. Sitting on the rug in front of the sink, Jamie proceeded to bang cups against mugs in a noisy symphony.

"You're good with him," Clay observed when she sat back down.

"I'm learning. Every day is a new experience. A new lesson." Many of them hard.

"At least you've had the opportunity these last, what? Fourteen months. I've missed out on everything."

She swallowed. Now that the moment had come to reveal the whole, horrible truth, she was having second thoughts. Clay was already angry with her. He might try to obtain custody of Jamie by proving her to be an unfit mother. He might win for, in her mind anyway, she was indeed the worst mother on the planet.

Lying to Clay and everyone else was the only way she could protect herself. Protect Jamie.

Her mind in a whirl, she opened her mouth, ready to blurt some concocted story. Clay's eyes stopped her cold. They were no longer ablaze with anger but filled with sadness and grief.

He truly regretted those missing fourteen months with Jamie.

Sierra's own heart shattered. Could she have been any crueler? She'd done to Clay exactly what the Stevensons had done to her—stolen a child from his parent.

"I've missed out on everything, too." Tears

pricked her eyes, and she brushed them away. "Except for the last three weeks."

"What are you talking about?"

There was no easy way to say it, no way to soften the crushing blow she was about to deliver. "I gave Jamie up for adoption when he was born. Last month, on January twenty-third—" she'd remember that day always "—he was returned to me."

His expression darkened. "I don't understand."

"I gave him up for adoption. His…caretakers—" she refused to use the word *parents*, even with *adoptive* in front of it "—changed their mind and returned him to me."

"You gave him up?" Clay recoiled in disbelief.

To Sierra, it felt like a slap.

"Why? How could you?"

Good question, and one she'd asked herself a thousand times.

"I was ill all during my pregnancy. Really ill. Day and night."

"That's no reason."

"I was also an emotional wreck. I took the news of your marriage hard." Boy, that was an understatement. "Maybe because I was pregnant, things overwhelmed me. I was alone. I didn't think I could confide in my family. My job didn't pay that well, had minimal benefits, and I was required to travel ten days a month. I wanted Jamie, truly I did. I just didn't know how I was going to manage everything."

"So, you decided not keeping your baby was easier."

The disgust in his voice cut her to the bone and echoed her own feelings about herself. This was why she hadn't come home before or confided in her family.

"It didn't happen like that. I was vulnerable, physically and emotionally weak. Confused and scared. I don't remember when my boss Ken first approached me about adopting Jamie. He was subtle, dropping tiny hints here and there, letting me get used to the idea slowly. The next thing I knew, I was in my last trimester and meeting with him and his wife and their attorney in order to finalize the adoption."

"You had to understand what was going on."

"I did understand." Sierra shoved her fingers through her hair. She'd gone over this again and again in her head, tried to justify what she'd done. So far, she hadn't. How could she expect Clay to understand? "They were very persuasive and nice. Or so I thought. Ken and Gail had been married twelve years and spent most of them trying to have a child. I was sure they'd be good parents, give Jamie a better life than I ever could. They helped me, supported me, paid my medical bills. I believed they wanted what was best for my baby. I didn't realize they were manipulating me."

"You wouldn't have had to go through that if you'd told me you were pregnant."

His sanctimonious attitude irritated her. "That's easy for you to say now that you're divorced."

"You're right," he admitted grudgingly.

"Believe me, I regretted my decision the moment I handed Jamie over to the Stevensons in the hospital."

"Why didn't you tell them you'd changed your mind?"

"I signed an agreement. And I was still convinced they'd be better parents than me."

"What happened?"

"Instead of getting my old life back or my new life together, I fell apart. Guilt, regret, remorse, you name it. Every aspect of my life suffered. I hit rock bottom and was about to lose my job, my apartment, friends, probably my family. I thought of hiring my own attorney, something I should have done in the first place, and seeing if I could get Jamie. Not long after that, Ken and Gail contacted me out of the blue. They didn't want Jamie anymore."

"What?"

"Gail had finally gotten pregnant. With twins. She was almost eight months along. Guess they were like those childless couples you hear about. They adopt, and suddenly the woman conceives."

"That's no reason to give back your child." Clay sounded as appalled and disgusted as Sierra had been. "He's not a shirt you decide you don't like once you get it home from the store."

"Gail said they never really bonded with him. And now that they were having their own biological children, they thought they'd give me first shot before their attorney arranged another adoption. She said they were also concerned about the baby's father."

"Me?"

"You didn't sign off on the adoption, which is usually required. Ken and Gail's attorney had advised them not to go ahead without your signature, but they were desperate and willing to take the chance you wouldn't appear one day. That changed when she got pregnant."

"And you decided to come home."

"I quit my job, gave up my apartment, cashed in my 401K and headed here. Now that I have Jamie, nothing or no one is going to take him from me again."

"I see," Clay said in a tone that made Sierra think he didn't see at all.

"I've been given a second chance, Clay. An opportunity to correct all the mistakes I made." The hell with her pride. She'd plead with him if that was what it took.

"Do those mistakes include not telling me?"

"I'm here now, and I've explained everything."

"Have you?"

Everything except the part where I fell in love with you. "Yes."

Jamie promptly abandoned the mugs and cups and waddled over to Sierra. She gathered him to her and kissed the top of his downy blond head.

Clay watched them. "We're going to have to come to an agreement about him."

"All right."

She'd let him visit Jamie at the ranch. A few times a week if he wanted. Then later, say next year, when she'd conquered her separation anxiety, Clay could take Jamie for the afternoon or maybe the whole day. Assuming she was still in Mustang Valley. She'd need a new job and these days a decent one was hard to find. Chances were she'd have to look outside the Scottsdale area, possibly outside the state.

"I'm glad you agree." Clay stood, went over to Jamie and patted his head, his smile tender and, this was a surprise to Sierra, almost fatherly. "I'll have my attorney contact you this week regarding the custody agreement."

"Custody agreement? Don't you mean visitation?" Sierra also stood, Jamie holding on to her leg.

Clay reached for Jamie, hefted him into his arms. "I want joint custody of our son."

"No! Forget it."

"We're going to raise him together, whether you like it or not."

She didn't like it. She didn't like it one bit.

Chapter Three

Clay rang his mother's doorbell. She always told him to use his key and just come in, but he didn't feel right about that. Perhaps because the spacious townhouse in the upscale Scottsdale neighborhood had never struck him as home.

His *mother's* home, he reminded himself.

The door swung open. "Clay, sweetheart! Come in." Blythe Duvall kissed his cheek. "I'm so glad you called. What a perfect way to spend a Saturday afternoon."

He gave her a fond squeeze before releasing her. "How are you, Mom?"

"Great. I shot an eighty-seven this morning. My best game in months."

All this time, and it still surprised him to see her in golfing attire. Or in the business suits and heels she wore to the title company where she worked as an escrow officer. She should be in jeans and boots and the floppy straw hat she'd refused to give up till it literally fell apart on her head.

Except she hadn't lived on a ranch in more than eight years and probably wouldn't ever again.

"Good for you." Clay followed her into the kitchen where a newspaper lay spread open on the breakfast bar.

"Can I get you something? A cold drink? Coffee?"

"Just ice water."

"You sounded so serious on the phone." She busied herself pouring their water. "Something the matter?"

"Not exactly."

He sat on a stool at the breakfast bar and let his gaze travel the stylish, ultra-contemporary kitchen, with its high-tech appliances and built-in flat-panel TV. Like his mother's clothes, the kitchen felt wrong. He remembered her cooking hearty meals at their huge gas range and a refrigerator covered with photos, reminder notes and school papers.

His parents had divorced about the time his father exercised a small-print clause in his contract with the Powells and sold off their land, effectively putting them out of the cattle business. Clay honestly didn't know if the sale of the land was the final straw in a marriage circling the drain or a last-ditch effort to save it.

The story changed depending on which parent was telling it.

Because his mother sided with Clay against his father regarding the Powells' land, they had remained close. Neither of them kept much of a connection with Bud Duvall.

"I have some news," Clay said. "Rather incredible news."

"Uh-oh." The twinkle in her eyes dimmed, replaced by worry. "The last incredible news you had was when you told me you and Jessica were getting married and moving to Texas."

They both knew how badly that had turned out. No two people had been more ill-suited for each other or more blind until it was too late.

"No, I'm not getting married again."

"What is it then?" She placed two glasses of ice water on the breakfast bar and slipped into the stool beside him.

He hesitated, honestly not sure how his mother would react. She wanted grandchildren. She also wanted Clay happily married and settled first.

"I told you Sierra Powell was coming home for the wedding."

"You did."

Clay's mother and Sierra's mother had been good friends before tragedy had struck, cutting Louise Powell's life short.

"She brought her young son with her."

"Really! I wasn't aware she had any children."

"No one was, including her family."

His mother's hands flew to her cheeks. "That must have come as a shock. Though I'm sure Wayne is overjoyed. He dotes on his granddaughter, Sage's daughter, too."

"He is overjoyed." Clay inhaled deeply. "There's something else you need to know. It's good news, I assure you. But unexpected."

"Now you've got me scared."

"Sierra's son... Well, I'm the father."

His mother stared at him blankly for several seconds. "How in the world did that happen?"

"The usual way."

"You haven't seen her since her mother died."

"I have. Two years ago when she came home for a visit. We didn't tell anyone. We thought it wise, considering how her family felt about me, us, at the time."

"You cheated on Jessica with Sierra?"

"No. Jessica and I were on the outs. I ran into Sierra at the Corner Diner. We got to talking, hit it off, and one thing led to another."

He summarized his brief affair with Sierra and what she'd told him about her pregnancy, Jamie's birth, adoption and getting him back.

"I can't believe it." His mother's happy smile warmed Clay. "I'm a grandmother. Wait till I tell—" She stopped, covered her mouth. "What am I saying? Poor Sierra. Such a terrible ordeal for her to go through."

Her? What about him? "She kept my son from me!"

"You dumped her."

"It wasn't like that."

"It was entirely like that. No wonder she was hurt and confused."

"She had no right to pawn Jamie off on strangers."

"We're all guilty of making bad decisions we later regret."

True. Clay was a walking, talking example. "I told her I want joint custody of Jamie."

"Is she agreeable?"

Clay thought back to how he and Sierra had parted yesterday at Ethan's apartment and her vehement protests. "She'd prefer I start with supervised visitation. I told I have no intention of being an every-other-weekend father."

His mother reached over and covered his hand with hers. "Please don't take this the wrong way, sweetheart, but why not?"

"I've always wanted kids. That was one of the reasons Jessica and I divorced."

"I remember how devastated you were when she miscarried."

"She didn't want children, Mom. She couldn't have been more relieved." Clay was the one who'd grieved over the loss. When he'd discovered not long after that Jessica was secretly taking birth control pills, their shaky marriage had rapidly deteriorated. "This is a second chance for me."

"I worry that you're so busy. You work seven days a week at the rodeo arena. You're at Powell Ranch at least two days a week helping Gavin with the stud and breeding business. And then there's the wild-mustang sanctuary. How are you going to fit raising a child, a *young* child at that, into your life?"

"I'll hire more help if necessary."

"I suppose you could."

"What happened to the happy grandmother?"

"I'm thrilled, of course. And I've always liked Sierra. It's just such a huge responsibility and an enormous adjustment. I think the two of you should proceed slowly. Whatever decisions you make must be best for everyone, especially little Jamie. Let him get used to Sierra before you start taking him."

His mother made sense, but Clay wasn't convinced. He had a lot of catching up to do with Jamie.

"Would you like to see him?"

She brightened. "I can't wait."

"Let's go over there now."

"This second?"

"Sure."

"Shouldn't you call Sierra first?"

"She's already expecting me. I told her yesterday I'd be by."

"But not that you'd be bringing me."

"You're Jamie's grandmother."

"Have you told your father yet?"

He shook his head.

"Don't you think you should?"

"I will. Later this week." Clay may be at odds with Bud, but he wouldn't deny the man his grandson. Not like Sierra had denied him.

"Tell you what." Blythe hopped off her stool. "You call Sierra while I change into slacks."

Two minutes later, Clay was shutting the Arcadia door behind him as he went onto his mother's back patio to make the call. He didn't want her hearing the conversation in case Sierra gave him more grief.

She answered the house phone on the second ring.

"It's Clay."

"Oh, hi."

He ignored her lack of enthusiasm. "I should be there in about a half-hour, forty-five minutes tops."

"It's not a good time. Jamie's napping."

"He'll wake up eventually. Won't he?"

"Yes—"

"We can wait."

"We?"

"My mother's coming with me."

Silence followed.

"We won't stay too long, I promise."

"All right. But in the future, I need more than a moment's notice you're bringing someone with you."

"She's my mother."

"Even so."

"Until we hammer out the custody agreement, I'm going to see Jamie every day. I'm more than willing to work out a schedule that's convenient for both of us."

"You don't get to dictate all the rules, Clay." There was an unaccustomed edge to her tone.

"Neither do you. Not anymore."

He heard her sharp intake of breath.

"Fine, I'll see you shortly." She hung up without saying goodbye.

Clay refused to get angry. This was only the beginning of a potentially long battle, since Sierra was intent on resisting him at every turn.

Unless...

The idea that had suddenly sprang to his mind quickly grew into a full-fledged plan.

And Clay liked having plans.

"You okay, Sierra?"

She glanced up to see her future sister-in-law Sage enter the kitchen wearing her khaki uniform. She was a field agent for the Arizona Game and Fish Department and often worked on the weekends. Later, as her pregnancy advanced, she'd be assigned to a desk job.

"I'm fine." Sierra moved away from the wall phone. "Clay and his mother are coming over."

"From the look on your face, I'd say that's bad."

"I was hoping for more time alone with Jamie before pulling him in a dozen different directions."

"Kids are resilient and do better with change than we think they will. Especially at his age."

"You're probably right." She *was* right, Sierra thought. It was her and not Jamie who needed more time.

Sage reached into the refrigerator and came away with a piece of leftover pizza, which she then placed on a paper plate and put in the microwave.

"Miss lunch?"

"No." She smiled embarrassedly. "I'm just always hungry."

"Lucky you. I spent most of my pregnancy throwing up or feeling like I wanted to."

"You're also lucky."

"I am, but what are you referring to?"

The previous evening, after Clay had left, Sierra had finally unloaded the entire story about Jamie to her family. They were supportive, sad she'd gone through so much misery alone and ecstatic she and Jamie were reunited. They also didn't quite understand her reasons for not telling them about her pregnancy from the start and, at least in Gavin's case, were a little mad at her.

"You're lucky Jamie's father wants to be part of his life," Sage said.

Sierra leaned her back against the counter and watched Sage devour her warmed-up pizza. "I'm okay with Clay being part of his life. It's his need to control that bothers me."

"Wanting to see their sons every day is natural for most dads. I wish my ex wanted to see Isa. Not for my sake, mind you. For hers. Gavin is wonderful and a hundred times the father my ex will ever be, but Isa still asks about her daddy and can't help feeling rejected. Jamie won't ever experience that."

The advice was good, and Sierra appreciated it. When she'd first got Jamie back, Sierra hadn't thought ahead to when he might ask about his father. Certainly not about what she'd say to him or how it would affect him. Now it was irrelevant. Jamie would know his father. Very well, if Clay had anything to do with it.

"I just wish he'd calm down a little. Quit trying to run the show."

"That's Clay for you."

"Is it?" Sierra really didn't know him, not the adult Clay. The youth and teenager she'd grown up with had been a lot like her older brothers. Competitive, confident, a talented athlete and enormously popular with the girls. The Clay she'd spent time with two years ago had been vulnerable and wounded and un-afraid to show his gentler side. That was the man she'd fallen in love with.

"He's a really good person, Sierra." Sage smiled fondly. "Hardworking, loyal, caring and sweet."

Sweet?

"He's not hard on the eyes, either," Sage added with an appreciative sigh. "You could do worse."

"We're not… There's nothing between us," Sierra protested.

"There was at one time."

Jamie's I'm-awake-where-are-you? cry carried through the house from the bedroom. "Oops." Sierra excused herself with a smile. "Someone's up from their nap."

"And demanding your attention. Isn't that just like a man? Big or little."

Jamie's crying stopped the moment Sierra stepped into the bedroom. He stood up in the portable crib, clinging to the side. One good growth spurt, and he'd be tall enough to crawl out on his own. She was going to have to buy a full-size crib soon, though she couldn't imagine where she'd put another piece of furniture in here.

She and Jamie needed their own place. Though she loved her family, she couldn't live *with* them and *off* them for long. Her pride wouldn't let her. In order to obtain her own place, however, she'd need a job. In order to get a job, she'd have to conquer her fear of being away from Jamie.

The solution was obvious. Find employment she could do from home.

That, she decided, would be the first order of business on Monday morning. She'd update her résumé and start sending it out. In the meantime, she'd offer to help around the ranch. Run errands. Answer the phone. Paperwork. Clean stalls if necessary, so long as she could have Jamie with her.

"Hungry, handsome?"

She hummed to Jamie as she combed his

rumpled hair. He patted her face and made kissing sounds; at least, Sierra chose to believe they were kissing sounds.

For a moment, she lost herself in the miracle of her son and forgot all about his father coming over. It didn't last. No sooner did she walk back into the kitchen, Jamie toddling along beside her, then she remembered.

She'd just finished giving him a snack of juice and Cheerios, when a knock sounded.

"Sierra! It's wonderful to see you again." The hug Blythe Powell gave Sierra when she opened the door was warm and genuine and a good ten seconds long.

Her resistance melted. Here was someone from her past, an important someone. In a small way, hugging Blythe was like hugging her mother again.

Suddenly, Sierra wanted Jamie to meet his only living grandmother.

"Come in." Her pleasure was cut short when Clay sauntered into the kitchen.

He was carrying an old-fashioned wooden rocking horse, one that had been ridden hard and loved well, given the worn paint and frayed yarn mane. Once inside, he set it in the middle of the floor.

"I hope you don't mind I brought this

along," Blythe explained. "It was Clay's when he was Jamie's age. His grandfather made it for him."

The grandfather she'd named Jamie after? Yes, she thought, observing Clay's features soften.

"Is this him?" Blythe approached Jamie, her hands clasped in front of her, her face an explosion of joy.

Jamie, excited over the commotion, started slapping the tray on his high chair.

"Hello there." Blythe bent so that her face was on Jamie's level. "Aren't you adorable?"

His eyes went huge, and his mouth started quivering.

"Goodness gracious, don't cry."

Sierra rushed over. "He's a little shy around new people."

Except when it came to Clay.

"It's okay," Blythe crooned, not appearing the least bit offended. "We'll get to know each other slowly."

Sierra removed Jamie from the high chair and bounced him in her arms, standing next to Blythe so he could get used to her. After a minute, he settled down. The next minute, he was reaching for Blythe's glasses.

She captured his hand, put it to her lips and

blew a raspberry on his palm. Jamie snatched his hand back, stared at it in amazement, burst into giggles, then pushed it into her face.

"Ma, ma, ma."

Tears sprang to Blythe's eyes, and she laughed along with Jamie. "He looks just like Clay did as a baby."

Sierra didn't deny the resemblance, though she sometimes thought she saw some of her father in him, too.

After another two minutes and another dozen raspberries, Jamie was more than willing to go to his grandmother. She took him gratefully.

"Do you mind?" she asked, indicating the chair where Sierra had been sitting when they arrived.

"Sit, please." She caught Clay's glance and was struck still.

The sweetness Sage had referred to earlier shone in his expression. "Thank you," he mouthed.

She shrugged, ignoring the mild thrum of her heartstrings.

"Can I get you something?" she offered.

"I'm fine." Blythe and Jamie were engaged in a game of peek-a-boo.

"Me, too." Clay removed his cowboy hat

and set it on the counter. At the table, he stroked Jamie's head. "The rest of the family out working?"

"Yes." Saturdays, as Sierra was learning, were the busiest days of the week for the Powell Riding Stables and Gavin's stud and breeding business. "Ethan's shoeing horses, and Gavin said something about new brood mares arriving. If you want to go talk to them, your mother and I—"

"I want to talk to you."

All the warm, cozy feelings Sierra had been having promptly vaporized. "Right this minute?"

"Mom can watch Jamie."

Blythe must have heard them, but she didn't look away from Jamie.

"I haven't hired an attorney yet," Sierra said softly.

"It's not that kind of conversation."

What kind was it, then? She'd much prefer stalling, except he would push and push and not relent until she did.

"We can sit in the living room."

"I was thinking of somewhere more private. Like the back patio."

"No. I can't see Jamie from outside." She couldn't see him from the living room, either, but he would be only one room away, and she could hear him. That would minimize her anxiety.

"Mom's not going to—"

"Of course she's not."

"Then why?"

"It's the living room or not at all."

Sierra couldn't explain her phobia to herself, much less other people. Losing Jamie had made her overprotective and unreasonably afraid. She would, she was convinced, improve in time. Everyone just needed to be patient with her.

"Okay." He led the way.

Sierra chose the chair closest to the hallway.

Rather than sit, Clay stood at the large picture window, studying the courtyard, beyond which lay Mustang Valley and the community of Mustang Village at its center.

He was, Sierra grudgingly admitted, a nice-looking man. Tall, broad-shouldered, lean-hipped and with a ruggedly handsome profile. His jeans were the same everyday brand her brothers wore. Not so his Western-cut shirt. She'd bet if she viewed the label inside the collar it would bear a designer name. His quality leather boots and belt were hand-tooled by expert craftsmen.

According to her brothers' account, Clay toiled laboriously running his various business ventures. He was apparently doing well.

A memory stirred of her nestled beside that tall frame, her fingertips stroking that rugged profile as early-morning light streamed in through the shutters. Even as she shoved the memory aside, a flush crept up her neck to her cheeks.

He abruptly turned, startling her, and she averted her head before he noted her flummoxed state.

When he sat, it was in the chair adjacent to hers, his knees separated from hers by mere inches.

"I don't want to make this difficult on you," he started, his voice low.

"I thought you said we weren't going to discuss Jamie's custody."

"We're not. Well, not the legal aspect of it."

"What then?"

He exhaled slowly. "Promise me you'll consider what I say before going ballistic."

"I don't go ballistic."

"You did a little yesterday and just now when I suggested we talk on the back patio."

"I told you, I get nervous when Jamie's out of my sight."

"Which is why I've been rethinking my paternity suit."

Thank goodness!

Her shoulders sagged with relief. "I swear to you, I'll be very generous with visitation."

"Oh, I still want custody of Jamie."

"What!" She sat up. "Not on your life."

"Not full custody."

Her patience snapped, and she pushed to her feet. "Quit playing games with me."

"Sit back down and listen."

She'd never heard him talk so sharply. Reluctantly, she lowered herself into the chair.

"Joint custody is more than shuffling a child between two residences. It's co-parenting. Both of us working as a team to raise our son. To do that successfully, we need to spend as much time together as possible. The three of us."

"Define *as much time as possible*."

"I'd rather define *together*."

"Go on."

"Twenty-four/seven."

"Forget it," Sierra bit out.

"Would you rather I take Jamie half the time? I will."

The thought of Clay taking Jamie for even

an hour had her—how had he put it?—going ballistic.

"You can't stay here. There isn't enough room." If he thought he was sharing her bed, he was crazy.

"I agree." He leaned forward, pinning her in place with his unyielding gaze. "Which is why you and Jamie are going to live with me."

Chapter Four

Sierra would have liked to think she'd heard Clay incorrectly, except she hadn't.

"You say *going to live with you* like I don't have a choice."

"You do have a choice. Many of them, in fact. I just happen to think living with me is the best one under the circumstances."

He straightened in his chair, calm and cool and collected. Not one neatly trimmed hair sticking sideways or one droplet of perspiration dotting his brow. Her hair, on the other hand, was a mess, the result of constantly shoving her fingers through the thick strands. And the sweat-soaked collar of her shirt stuck to the back of her neck, intensifying her discomfort.

"Best for you," she snapped.

"For all of us. Jamie will have the benefit of both parents raising him, and you'll get to be with him most of the time."

As opposed to separated from him *half* the time, if Clay won his paternity suit.

Sierra already ached with loneliness. "I don't want to uproot him again. He's just getting used to me. To this place."

"You've been here…what? All of two days? I can't imagine he's become that attached."

"No." She shook her head. "I won't do it."

Clay continued talking as if he hadn't heard her. "The rodeo arena isn't far from here, only a couple of miles. You can visit your family whenever you want or they can come over. Ethan's at the arena almost every day as it is, and Gavin once a week."

"You live at the rodeo arena?"

"Sometimes it feels like that, I'm there so much."

Not a place she saw herself either residing or bringing up her son. Too far from town. Too dangerous, what with horses and bulls and vehicles everywhere. It was probably also dusty and dirty. San Francisco was hardly perfect, but she'd resided there for the last seven years and grown accustomed to city life.

"The house is actually on the next parcel over," Clay continued. "I built it shortly after the arena was finished."

There were so many reasons to refuse his offer besides uprooting Jamie. She picked the first one.

"I've never shared a house or apartment with a man, and I won't unless he and I are in a committed relationship."

"I respect your principles, and I wouldn't ask you to compromise them."

Oh, okay. She hadn't expected him to give in so quickly. "Well, I guess there's no need—"

"I built a casita behind the house. It's not large, basically a bedroom, a sitting area and a bathroom. But you and Jamie could be comfortable there. You'd have to take some of your meals in the main house. With me," he added, his tone such that Sierra clearly understood shared meals were part of the deal.

"I can't live off you. It wouldn't be right."

"I'll be paying monthly child support for Jamie. Any rent, if you want, can be considered part of that support."

"It still feels like a handout."

"Fine. You can work for me."

"This is no joke."

"I'm not joking. I need the help."

She eyed him suspiciously. "With what? I was an assistant sales rep for a medical-supply company. I haven't been on a horse since…three years ago last Christmas."

Like the rest her family, Sierra had grown up on and around horses, but she had abandoned the cowboy lifestyle at seventeen when she'd left for college. What possible job could there be at a rodeo arena that didn't involve knowledge of livestock, expertise with a rope and excellent horsemanship skills?

"Office work mostly," Clay said. "Answering phones, correspondence, paying bills and depositing checks, livestock-rental contracts, maintaining liability waivers and promoting jackpot events."

That actually didn't sound too bad and like something Sierra might even enjoy, especially promotion. She was good with people and liked working with them. It was what had once made her the go-to assistant sales rep.

She could be that kind of worker again.

Wait a minute! Even if she could leave Jamie all day, she wasn't working for Clay. Not in this lifetime.

"You've thought of everything, haven't you?"

"I haven't. Which is why I need to run this by my attorney so he can draw up an employment contract."

She almost laughed. "You not only expect Jamie and I to live with you, you want me to sign a contract?"

"All my employees do."

She gaped at him. "How long are these contracts for?"

He didn't miss a beat. "One year."

"I can't put my life on hold that long."

"I'm not going to chain you to me." One corner of his wide mouth tipped up as if he were about to smile.

Did the idea appeal to him?

"What if I want to take a trip?"

"You can leave Jamie with me."

"Leave him?" Impossible. Clay *was* chaining her to him. "This is ridiculous."

"I disagree. It's a very fair arrangement."

"You're trying to manipulate me. And Jamie. Trying to force us to do what you want by threatening to take him away from me."

"Joint custody isn't taking him away from you."

It was. For seven out of fourteen days.

Hard to believe she'd once fallen in love with this…this…control freak?

"Talk it over with your family," he said, "and your attorney, when you retain one. Send me his or her name, and I'll have mine forward the documents."

"How long do I have to decide?" she asked snidely.

Clay ignored her tone. "A week."

"That's not enough time!"

"Ten days, then."

"Be reasonable."

His voice remained level, though his jaw muscles tightened. "I'm being far more reasonable with you than you were with me."

He was getting back at her. She didn't think he'd stoop so low.

Then again, she had done a terrible thing to him. He could sue for full custody, and he wasn't. She should be grateful for that, at least.

Sierra frowned. Come Monday morning, she wouldn't be sending out her résumé, she'd be finding an attorney to represent her.

Jamie suddenly let out a high-pitched squeal, and she shot out of her chair. How could she have forgotten about him for—what?—five minutes? No, seven. She dashed into the kitchen, Clay hot on her heels.

Jamie was sitting on the rocking horse, Blythe kneeling on the floor beside him.

Sierra came to a stop beside them, her breathing shallow. "What happened?"

"Jamie caught his shoe on the foot peg. When I stopped him from rocking in order to unwedge his shoe, he began squealing."

That was all? Sierra stroked Jamie's head to reassure herself.

His fingers gripping the hand pegs and feet properly positioned, he took off galloping again—which consisted of rocking the horse as fast as he could, his angelic face aglow.

Blythe watched him, her hand hovering protectively.

Sierra considered stepping in and lifting Jamie from the rocking horse. A part of her was angry enough at Clay to do it. But she'd never seen her son having so much fun.

Clay stepped around her, retrieved his hat from the counter and dropped it onto Jamie's head. Too large for him, it immediately fell forward over his eyes.

"Ride 'em, cowboy." Pride and affection

shone in Clay's eyes. He tipped the hat back so Jamie could see.

Father, son and grandmother all laughed.

Sierra stood motionless, her emotions in a tangle.

This was the man she'd fallen in love with two years ago. The man who'd allowed her to dream of the impossible.

He was also the same man who'd broken her heart and left her miserable enough to make the biggest mistake of her life.

She would, she realized, have to guard her heart ruthlessly because it would be much too easy to fall in love with him again.

"I really appreciate you seeing me on such short notice." Sierra slipped into the visitor's chair, settled Jamie on her lap and looked across the desk at her attorney.

"No problem. I understand the urgency." Roberto Torres was Sage's cousin-in-law. He'd represented Sage during her custody dispute with her ex, and she'd highly recommended him to Sierra.

"Did Clay's attorney send over the papers?" She'd filled Roberto in on the situation during their phone call that morning.

"He did." Roberto picked up a stack of papers on his desk and passed several sheets to Sierra. "Here's a copy of the paternity suit and a proposed joint-custody agreement. I've only had time to skim both documents."

Sierra attempted to read the first page of the custody agreement but nothing made sense. It was the turmoil raging inside her and not the legalese that tripped her up. She'd been back in Mustang Valley a total of four days and, other than her family welcoming her home, nothing had gone as planned.

Blythe Duvall couldn't have been nicer or more considerate on Saturday, which Sierra appreciated. Things between her and Clay, however, had remained tense, continuing through yesterday evening when he'd stopped by the ranch while the family was having dessert. She expected more of the same when he visited today, especially as he knew she was meeting with her attorney.

"The terms of the custody agreement are pretty standard." Roberto laid down the papers. "You mentioned on the phone this isn't what you want."

"No, but I'm not sure I have a choice. I'm worried Clay will sue for full custody if I don't cooperate." Sierra held the papers out of Jamie's curious grasp. "Can he get it?"

"Probably not."

"But I gave Jamie up for adoption. Clay could use that against me. You said the attorney he hired is one of the best."

"You're not an unfit mother, Sierra, which is what he'd have to prove. Joint custody, however, is almost a given."

Sierra's hopes, small to begin with, plummeted. "What's this 5-2-2-5 parenting time schedule?"

"Basically, it's alternating weekends. A fourteen-day schedule that continually repeats."

"Sounds complicated." And awful.

"I'm told you get used to it, and that it's easier than a 7-7 schedule," he added kindly.

"What if I refuse?"

"The judge will likely order it."

And Clay wins again.

"I hate this feeling of helplessness," she said through clenched teeth.

"We can always try and negotiate the terms. Propose working up to the 5-2-2-5 schedule slowly."

"Clay won't do it."

"Let's ask. You'll feel less helpless if you have some say."

She flipped through the pages as best she

could with Jamie in the way. "What else do you recommend?"

"A review of the schedule in three months to determine how well it's working and every six months thereafter. Also, what happens when Jamie's sick? Or you're sick? Or Clay? Grandparent visitations? Vacations—yours and his? Business trips? Babysitting? Day care? Preschool?"

Sierra wished Roberto would talk more slowly.

"I'm not sure about this employment contract," he said, pulling a sheet out.

"Employment contract?" She shuffled through the papers in her lap, dropping some. "I never agreed to work for him."

"No?"

"He mentioned it, but I didn't say yes."

"Well, I strongly advise you consider carefully before accepting. Living in his casita is one thing—"

"I'm not working for him," she stated flatly.

"All right then." He set several pages aside. "I won't review the employment contract."

Sierra fumed. Of all the nerve. She was ready to tell Clay he could shove the whole paternity suit where the sun didn't shine. Except that would gain her nothing and would quite possibly make matters worse.

Another thought occurred to her. "Will me not having a job hurt my chances?"

"I don't believe so. Are you currently looking?"

"I've just started. I'm hoping to find something I can do from home."

"We'll ask for day care costs. Keep in mind Clay will also need day care on his days with Jamie. You might want to use the same person or facility as him. Easier on Jamie that way."

"I'm not putting Jamie in day care. I can't."

Roberto gazed at her curiously, waiting for her to explain.

"I have trouble being separated from him. Even for short periods of time." *Like a few minutes.* "I thought I'd lost him forever. Since getting him back..." She hugged Jamie, her throat tight. "I'm scared to death of losing him again. I know it's completely unreasonable, but I can't help myself. That's why joint custody is, well, impossible for me. Can't we please start with visitation?"

"All we can do is ask."

Sierra bit back a sob.

"I've met Clay. He's not a bad guy. Have you talked to him about your apprehensions?"

"A little. That's why he suggested Jamie and I move into the casita."

Roberto reached into his desk drawer, withdrew a business card and handed it to her. "I'd like to make another suggestion. If I'm out of line, I apologize, but remember, I'm your advocate and only want what's best for you and Jamie."

She took the card and stiffened when she read the name of a psychologist on it.

"It's completely understandable for someone in your position, who's been through what you have, to suffer anxieties. Learning to cope with them will only improve things for you and Jamie." He waited while she flipped the card around in her fingers. "Dr. Brewster is someone we frequently refer our clients to, and she's very good."

"I can't afford counseling."

"Clay can. We'll include counseling in the agreement, both individual sessions for you and joint ones."

"He and I together?"

"You want to successfully co-parent Jamie. To do that, you and Clay have to get along."

"I'm not going to ask him to pay for counseling sessions. He might think I'm unbalanced and use it against me."

"The judge is going to order at least one counseling session, along with parenting classes. More sessions make sense and show you're trying your best to make the agreement work."

Sierra had her doubts. Could she trust Clay?

"Explore all your options," Roberto said. "Visit his home and check out the casita. See if you and Jamie could be comfortable living there before we go any further."

"I assure you, I won't be comfortable."

"Maybe, maybe not. You don't know till you look."

Sierra and Roberto continued to discuss the paternity suit for another twenty minutes, until Jamie tired. They agreed on a follow-up meeting the next afternoon.

She couldn't wait to get out of the attorney's office. She kept hearing the phrase *make the agreement work* over and over in her head as she walked through the building's main lobby and out the double glass doors.

Granted, she didn't want a joint-custody agreement with Clay. But this whole situation was starting to feel less like two people lovingly co-parenting their child and more like an impersonal business arrangement.

* * *

Clay watched from his front porch as Sierra pulled in beside his pickup truck and parked. Jogging down the steps, he headed for her car, intending to open her door. She was already at the rear hatch by the time he got there.

"You found the place."

"The signs along the road made it pretty easy." She removed a stroller and quickly set it up. For someone who'd been an active mother only one short month, she appeared to know what she was doing. "This is a busy place. I must have passed six horse trailers on my way in."

"There's a rodeo in Scottsdale next week. A lot of local cowboys are getting in as much practice as possible before then."

"That's what Ethan said."

She was being civil. On the verge of friendly. Not what he'd expected so soon following her appointment with her attorney. When she'd called him an hour ago and asked to see the casita, he'd stammered a surprised "How soon can you be here?"

He cautioned himself not to jump the gun. Her request didn't mean she'd changed her mind about living with him. But she was obviously entertaining the possibility, which was a huge step. Clay fully intended to obtain joint custody of his son. He'd rather accomplish it without battling Sierra.

"If you're interested, we can tour the rodeo facility and office when we're done here."

"Won't it be dark by then?" She pushed the empty stroller to the rear passenger door, then reached inside and lifted Jamie from his car seat.

"The floodlights will be on." Clay stood at her side, observing her every move. He had a lot to learn about caring for babies, too.

"Maybe." She set Jamie in the stroller. "I have an errand to run on the way home."

Jamie wiggled excitedly, and it took Sierra several attempts to get the safety straps buckled, his jacket zipped and his ball cap situated on his head.

Clay smiled and winked at his son and was rewarded with a silly giggle. Later, he would insist on holding Jamie. For now, Clay let Sierra be in charge.

"Do people always practice at night?" She handed Jamie his toy pony. For once, the boy disregarded it in favor of his surroundings.

"Depends," Clay said. "More often in the summer months when it's too hot during the day to ride. With the rodeo coming up, however, practice will last till midnight if I let it."

"Will you let it?" She tilted her head at an appealing angle.

Clay promptly forgot the question. "What? Oh, yeah. Practice. Probably not tonight. I don't have enough wranglers willing to stay late."

She took hold of the stroller's handle and released a foot brake. "Is Ethan here?"

"He is. We can watch him working the horses if you want."

"We'll see."

"That's right. You have an errand to run."

She didn't respond.

Clay wanted to ask her how her meeting with her attorney had gone but hesitated. Better to leave the joint-custody agreement to their respective representatives. He didn't want there to be any tension between him and Sierra while they were looking at the casita.

"You have a beautiful home." She took in the expansive grounds as they walked a shrub-lined footpath leading to the enclosed backyard.

"We can go inside when we're done with the casita. You'll like the kitchen. I designed it myself."

Would she like it? He realized after he'd made the comment he had no idea. He couldn't recall her spending much time in the kitchen as a teenager, and they'd either eaten out or grabbed a snack from the fridge during their brief affair.

Clearly she was wondering the same thing about him. Slanting him a curious look, she asked, "Do you cook?"

"When I have the time, which isn't often. I make the best country ribs and coleslaw you'll ever eat."

Funny, they could make a baby together and still not know the simplest things about each other.

"Hmm. I'm impressed." She carefully maneuvered the stroller over the uneven ground. "I haven't had ribs in years."

"Don't tell me. You're a vegan."

"No. I did try that once for a few months."

He could have sworn for just a second her mouth tipped up in a smile. His heart leapt. Maybe, possibly, the sense of humor that had charmed him two years ago hadn't entirely disappeared.

"This way." He gestured to their left to a small square building connected to the house by a wood-slat walkway. A small bridge rose at midpoint over the rocky bed of a natural wash.

Designed in the same Southwestern style as the main house right down to the red tile roof and carved oak door, the casita had its own private patio and a kiva fireplace with two wrought-iron chairs facing it. Leafy plants spilled over the sides of colorful ceramic pots placed on either side of the fireplace.

"The gate locks," Clay said, opening it so that they could enter the patio. "That way, Jamie can't get out. I'll also have extra dead bolt locks installed on both the casita's doors, high enough so he can't reach them. Right now, the heat's turned off, so it's a little cold inside."

Sierra didn't seem to notice that Clay was talking as though her moving in was a foregone conclusion.

She pushed the stroller through the front door and came to a sudden stop, her eyes wide. "It's bigger than it looks from the outside."

"Three hundred and sixty square feet altogether. I think the picture window and skylights give an illusion of spaciousness."

She continued past the recliner and queen-size bed to the tiny kitchen in the corner.

There, she ran her fingers along the edges of the single-basin sink and three-burner stove. Last, she opened the mini refrigerator for a quick peek at the contents, which consisted of a can of tomato juice and a box of baking soda.

"No oven," Clay said, "so you can't prepare a huge meal. But between the stovetop and the microwave, you and Jamie won't starve."

"There's always the meals we share with you."

She *would* bring up that condition.

Leaving the stroller outside the bathroom, she went in to explore. Clay was glad he'd spent the extra money and had a whirlpool tub installed.

"This is great," she exclaimed.

He smiled to himself.

Was she remembering that night they'd spent at the Phoenix Inn and their room with the built-in Jacuzzi? They'd drunk champagne and eaten strawberries amid swirling water and shared a continental breakfast in bed the next morning. In between, they'd made love. For hours.

Then, a week after Sierra went home, Jessica had crooked her little finger and Clay went right back to her like a trained lapdog.

Would he have been so eager if he'd known Sierra was pregnant?

Definitely not.

He'd have done right by Jamie, been a better father than his own ever was—*would* be a better father than his own. Put his family first, not his insatiable greed.

And he'd have done right by Sierra, too. Married her if that was what she'd wanted. Taken care of her, certainly.

What if she'd told him about the baby *after* he and Jessica had renewed their engagement? Would he have still married Jessica?

Clay was honest enough with himself to admit he had his doubts. Oh, he'd have still taken care of Jamie and Sierra. But left Jessica? Hard to say. The spell that woman cast on him had been strong *and* blinding.

"Da, da, da!"

Clay swung around. Had Jamie just called him Dada? He went to the stroller and knelt in front of his son, who wore an enormous grin and waved his pony in the air.

"Da, da, da, ba, ba."

"Hey, pal." Clay tugged on the brim of Jamie's ball cap, emotion thickening his voice. "I'm here."

"Hard consonants are easier to pronounce than soft ones." Sierra had stepped out of the bathroom and was standing beside Clay and Jamie. "They aren't necessarily words."

Guess Jamie wasn't calling him Daddy yet. "Is that what the baby books say?"

She blushed guiltily. "I have been reading up."

Clay stood and waited. After a moment, she met his gaze. They were closer than he'd first thought. So close the fronts of their jackets brushed. With the wall on one side and the stroller on the other, there was little room to maneuver, unless Sierra twisted and ducked into the bathroom.

She didn't.

Her eyes, a vivid blue and by far her most striking feature, held him immobile. He had only to lower his mouth a few inches and he'd be able to taste her lush pink lips. Slide his tongue over them until they parted and she leaned into him…

"Da, da, ba, da."

Clay jerked. What the heck just happened?

He was angry at Sierra. Furious. Didn't trust her. And with good reason. He was not in any way whatsoever attracted to her.

His pulse and sudden rapid breathing were making a liar of him.

Maybe her living in such close proximity wasn't a good idea after all.

Chapter Five

"We'd better get a move on." Sierra slipped gracefully out from between Clay and the wall. "I have that errand to run."

Clay watched her lean down to fix Jamie's loose shoe. The curve of her shapely posterior didn't go unnoticed.

Dang. If she could have escaped all along, why hadn't she?

Perhaps this zing of attraction from out of nowhere wasn't entirely one-sided.

Naw. She didn't look like a person who'd just been emotionally knocked to her knees. Her movements were too steady, her demeanor too cool.

Clay, on the other hand, was only now re-covering.

"Do you mind if I push Jamie?" Distractions. He needed distractions.

She hesitated.

"I admit, I don't have much experience but I think I can get him from here to the house without crashing."

"All right." She remained glued to his side, hovering with near obsessiveness as they left the casita.

"Any closer, and I'm going to run over you."

"Sorry."

Why had he opened his big mouth? Having her two feet away was infinitely less enjoyable than two inches.

The stroller wheels bumped over the wood slats as they walked to the house. Jamie laughed with delight, and Clay could imagine him saying, Again, Daddy, again.

They entered the house through a pair of French doors opening to a spacious great room. Clay found himself looking at the decidedly masculine decor through Sierra's eyes. Did she find the leather furniture, floor-to-ceiling bookcases and pool table too much?

"You were right." She went straight to the

kitchen with its antique buffet, plate racks and glass door cabinets. "It *is* fabulous." She turned in a half circle. "Look at that stove."

It was Clay's pride and joy. Six burners, a built-in grill, a conventional oven below and a convection oven above, the gas range had been designed to resemble one from the early 1900s.

She switched on a knob, and blue flames erupted from the front burner.

"You like to cook."

"When I get the chance. Same as you." The faint smile Clay had seen earlier in the casita reappeared and lasted two full seconds before fading.

Progress.

Jamie squawked and kicked his legs hard enough to shake the stroller.

"What's wrong?" Clay asked. If Jamie required changing, he'd do that, too, though he wasn't looking forward to it.

"I think he's tired of sitting."

That wasn't what had started Jamie fussing. He'd spied Oreo, who lumbered tiredly into the kitchen, his feathery tail wagging.

"Is that Oreo?" Sierra didn't wait for an answer. She reached down and scrunched the dog's ears in her hands. "He was old two years ago."

"Older now. Almost seventeen. He doesn't do much except move from one sleeping spot to the next."

And lick faces, present company included. Sierra laughed as she twisted her head out of Oreo's reach.

Jamie's kicking increased. "Da, da, da."

Great. His son was now calling his dog Daddy.

"His adoptive… The Stevensons had a dog," Sierra explained. "He's used to them."

"Go on, let them play. Oreo likes kids."

"Kids or babies? There's a difference."

"He's the gentlest dog in the world."

Oreo lived up to Clay's boasts. The moment Sierra set Jamie on the floor, he tumbled over to the old spaniel. Throwing his arms around Oreo's neck, he buried his face in the still-lustrous black-and-white coat and squealed excitedly.

Oreo's only reaction was to look up at Clay with a see-what-I-put-up-with-for-you expression on his face. Even when Jamie pulled on Oreo's fur, the dog's tail continued to wag.

"He *is* good with kids." Sierra smiled—*really* smiled.

The light radiating from it arrowed straight into Clay's chest. He wasn't sure he'd ever be the same.

He wasn't sure he wanted to be the same.

"I worry Jamie will get hurt." She nibbled her lip nervously. "He tried playing with Cassie's puppy Blue yesterday. It didn't go well. Jamie got too rambunctious."

"Did Blue snap at him?"

"No, no. Just yelped and scampered away. Which scared Jamie and he started crying."

"That won't happen with any dog of mine. Or horse."

"Just because Oreo's trustworthy doesn't mean you can put Jamie on a pony." She leveled a finger at Clay, her mouth set in a determined line. "Not happening, Clay Duvall. You hear me?"

How did she know he'd already contacted one of his livestock dealers about any ponies for sale?

"Not until he's older," she stated.

"How old?"

"Six, at least."

"I had my first pony at three."

"Three! Are you crazy?"

"If I don't buy him a pony, your dad or brothers will."

"No one is buying Jamie a pony."

Clay dropped the subject. For now. They'd compromise eventually. Clay was more concerned about Jamie living here with him.

And Sierra.

Taking both boy and dog with them, they toured the rest of the house. When they were done, they left for the arena. Oreo remained behind in the kitchen, to Jamie's acute disappointment. He wailed at being parted from his new best friend and didn't stop.

Clay hoisted Jamie into his arms, and the boy instantly quieted.

"That's better, pal."

Sierra pushed the empty stroller. "We can put him back now."

"He's fine."

She crinkled her brow. "You can't carry him all the way to the rodeo arena."

"Sure I can."

The horse operation was only about a hundred and fifty yards from the house. Close enough for Clay to keep watch on everything and far enough to afford him a modicum of privacy.

Sierra said nothing.

Jamie did. He would point to something that caught his attention, a horse and rider, a truck and trailer, one of the wranglers, and blurt a string of nonsense syllables as if he were commenting on what he saw.

Clay enjoyed every second and responded with "What do you think of that?" or "I know, it *is* big."

He observed the people they passed. Some openly stared. Clay waved or nodded, not minding the attention. He was proud to be a father. It was a feeling he treasured and, he glanced at Sierra, one he'd fight for if necessary.

"Most of the bulls, horses and calves are kept in pastures or paddocks over there." He indicated the acres and acres of open land behind the rodeo arena. "We transport them to the holding pens for practices and jackpot events. The maternity pastures are to the east."

"Maternity pastures?" Sierra asked showing the first hint of interest.

"Leasing livestock to rodeos is a large part of my business. Occasionally, I purchase livestock. Most often calves. For the larger stock, horses in particular, I've started breeding my own, which was one of the reasons I went into business with Gavin. I'm hoping Prince will produce quality bucking stock," he said, referring to the wild mustang he and Sierra's brothers had captured last fall. "I've bred him to three of my best mares."

"Hmm." Sierra's response was noncommittal but the spark remained in her eyes.

They watched the wranglers herd a new batch of bucking broncs to the holding pens. A few of the men were on foot, most on horseback, Ethan among them. When he was done and the bucking horses secured, he trotted over to Clay and Sierra and dismounted.

"Hey, buckeroo." Ethan poked Jamie on the nose. "Which of these bad boys are you going to ride tonight?"

Still in Clay's arms, Jamie grabbed for Ethan's horse. The big gelding was less enthused with the attention than Oreo had been and jerked back.

"He's not getting anywhere near a horse." Sierra planted herself between Clay and her brother, glaring at them both.

They exchanged glances and dutifully replied, "Yes, ma'am."

She harrumphed as if she didn't quite believe them.

While Clay and Ethan discussed the upcoming rodeo, Sierra kept watch on Jamie, ready to seize him from Clay if the horse got even one inch closer.

He decided to give her a break and handed Jamie over to her. Shoulders sagging with relief, she returned him to the stroller. Jamie objected loudly and pushed at the restraining bar.

"Cute kid," Ethan said to Clay. His manner had gone from lighthearted to serious.

"Yep, he is."

"Sissy told us about you wanting her and Jamie to move into the casita."

"I think it's a good compromise."

"You're my best friend, Clay. There isn't anyone else I want to stand up for me at my wedding next weekend."

Ethan's words warmed Clay. "I feel the same."

"The thing is, if you hurt my sister or her boy, it won't matter how good a friend you are."

Clay wasn't bothered by the thinly veiled threat. If he were in Ethan's shoes, he'd want to protect his sister and nephew, too.

"For the record, I don't plan on hurting either of them."

Ethan's grin, normally ear to ear, didn't reach his eyes. "Okay. Because I'd hate to have to hunt you down."

* * *

Sierra was too busy with Jamie to pay much attention to what Clay and her brother were saying. Something, however, must have changed for they were suddenly serious and, this was odd, posturing.

Really? Men!

She knelt down in front of Jamie so that their faces were on the same level.

"Hey there, handsome."

He ignored her, twisting his small body sideways to face Clay, his left arm extended.

"It's Mommy. Come on, look at me."

Jamie did, for a second. Then, his attention returned to Clay.

Not far away, a golden retriever stuck his head out of a parked truck window and barked.

"See the doggie, Jamie?"

He didn't care.

Sierra gave up and stood, not liking her son's fixation with Clay. She and Jamie were newly bonded, and she wanted to be the one he reached for. The one able to soothe him when he was distressed. The center of his small universe.

What would happen if—more likely, when—

Clay was granted joint custody? Sure, he was an eager parent now. More than eager, almost obsessive. That could change. The Stevensons had been eager parents in the beginning, too.

Sierra would do whatever was necessary to protect her son from hurt and rejection. But how?

Live and work here, she supposed. That would enable her to stay close to Jamie, including the days Clay had him. She might even be able to convince him to postpone taking Jamie overnight until they were more settled, and she was on firmer emotional ground.

Jamie's excited chatter alerted her to Clay's presence behind her.

"Sorry about that," he said, his apology directed at Sierra but his disarming smile all for Jamie.

And it *was* disarming. She'd basked in it often two years ago when, for a very short time, he'd forgotten all about Jessica.

Jamie's fidgeting returned Sierra to her senses. Thank goodness. She didn't need to be thinking about Clay's smile and how she'd basked in it.

Before she could dig Jamie's toy pony out of the diaper bag, Clay reached into his pocket and handed Jamie his set of keys.

He's learning, she thought. Clay might turn out to be a good father after all. Maybe even a better father than she was a mother.

Sierra bit down hard, determination overriding her insecurities. Jamie would love her so much he would never blame her for giving him up temporarily.

"Ready for the rest of the tour?" Clay asked.

She gripped the stroller handle and forced a smile. "Let's go."

He showed her the arena, bucking chutes, roping chutes and holding pens. Beside the bank of aluminum bleachers stood a two-story wooden structure with a staircase on the outside. Instead of windows, the second story was open on all four sides.

"Above is the announcer's stand." He opened a door on the ground floor and flipped on a light switch. "This is the first aid station."

She noted the room appeared well-equipped and neatly organized.

"It used to be my office, but I moved that to the barn after Caitlin started working for me."

Sierra had recently learned Ethan's fiancée, a licensed nurse, ran the first aid station for Clay during events. It was another reminder of how out of touch she'd become with her family.

She had to rectify that. She loved and needed her family. They would be all she had on the days Jamie spent with Clay.

"Can I see the office?" she asked, a heavy weight bearing down on her heart.

"Come on, I'll show you."

They started toward the barn. Other than being newer, it closely resembled the one at Powell Ranch.

Halfway there, Jamie started fussing again. Given that it was nearly six o'clock and two hours since he'd last eaten, he was probably hungry. She reached into the diaper bag. Too late, she remembered she was out of animal crackers.

"What's wrong with him?" Clay asked.

"He's hungry."

"Should we go back to the house and feed him?"

Prolonging her visit was the last thing she wanted. "He'll be okay if we don't take too long."

"He doesn't sound okay," Clay observed as Jamie's wailing gained conviction. "I have some instant oatmeal in the office."

"You eat breakfast in your office?"

"I like to tackle the paperwork before my day gets away from me."

Considering how late he'd worked the last two nights, he put in some mighty long hours.

They rounded the side of the barn. A flimsy plastic office sign was mounted beside a brown steel door.

Clay opened it.

Sierra made a face, recalling the barn office at her family's ranch with its perpetually grimy windows, scuffed floors and dust-blanketed desk. Not that she faulted her brothers. Who could keep an office clean in a barn?

Clay lifted the stroller's front wheels over the raised threshold. Jamie stopped whining—momentarily, Sierra was sure. If she'd learned anything about her son these last several weeks it was that he possessed a voracious appetite.

"Here we are."

Sierra prepared herself for the worst and stepped inside. She let out a small gasp. The office was not only spanking clean, it was attractive and housed state-of-the-art equipment. Framed photographs decorated the walls. A few featured Clay as a teenager, roping calves and riding bulls. Three photos were of the rodeo arena at various stages of construction. A large portrait of Prince hung over a cabinet.

As she had when she'd viewed his house,

Sierra found herself stammering as she commented, "This is nice."

"I'm not the most organized person in the world."

She'd barely noticed the piles of papers and folders on the desk. "Who does your office work now?"

"Me, mostly. I also use a temp agency. They send someone out once or twice a week."

Despite her conviction not to be, Sierra was curious. "How many hours a day do you think would be enough?"

"Four, for sure. Maybe more the week before an event. We have a bull-and-bronc-riding jackpot next month."

As they talked, Clay went to a cupboard where he removed a bowl and package of instant oatmeal. Using water from a cooler, he prepared the oatmeal and heated it in the microwave.

Sierra lifted Jamie from the stroller and sat with him in the visitor chair. A minute later, Clay handed her the bowl of oatmeal and a spoon. Jamie ate as if he was starving.

Clay sat behind the desk, facing them. "I hope we're not spoiling his dinner."

"Are you kidding? This is just the appetizer. He'll have the main course at home."

"You're really good with him."

She couldn't look at Clay, afraid he'd see the blush warming her cheeks. Why in the world did his praise embarrass her?

"Thanks. I'm trying."

"I'd like to try, too. Feeding him, that is."

"Now?" She didn't want to give up Jamie. "He's almost done."

"So I see." Clay chuckled. "He definitely has my appetite."

Clay did eat a lot, Sierra remembered that about him. One would never know it to look at him, however. He didn't appear to have an ounce of fat on his lean, athletic frame.

Enough already with the personal thoughts about Clay, Sierra chided herself. Their relationship was already confusing enough.

While Jamie played with the spoon, Clay rambled on about the day-to-day office operations. Sierra listened, wishing she didn't like the sound of the job so much. If not for having to leave Jamie with a caretaker, and Clay being her boss, it would be a perfect job for her. Flexible hours, lots of customer contact and a variety of duties, some easy, some challenging.

"Then there's the mustang sanctuary," he said. "We're moving it from your family's ranch to here. I'm donating the pasture space, water and any feed and medical care above and beyond donations. Your brothers will still supervise the training. I'd like to organize a wild-horse auction to raise awareness and, hopefully, money. We're running low. I'd also like to investigate any potential government grants. You could be in charge of that."

"What about Sage?"

Sierra's future sister-in-law had founded the sanctuary shortly after Prince's capture in order to place formerly unadoptable feral horses in good homes. It was her hobby and her passion.

"Between the wedding, her full-time job and the baby due this summer, she's had to step down. You'd make an excellent replacement."

Clay couldn't be holding a more tempting carrot in front of Sierra. Part of her former job had been planning client-appreciation luncheons, annual charity campaigns and employee retreats. She'd not only enjoyed the work, she'd shown a real knack for it.

"Babies are time-consuming," she agreed, thinking of those four-plus hours a day she'd be away from Jamie.

She didn't trust anyone to watch him, with

the exception of her family, and they were far too busy with their own lives and livelihoods for her to ask such a huge favor.

Better she decline Clay's offer and find a job she could do from home. Then, once she'd saved enough money, she could locate her own place—and be miserably alone on the days Clay had Jamie.

Unless she moved into the casita.

Resentment, a frequent companion recently, built inside her. Clay had done nothing. Nothing *more,* anyway, than offer her a charming place to live and a great job. Yet she felt pressured again.

"Is there a sink where I can wash this?" She rose from the chair, Jamie in one arm, the empty oatmeal bowl in her free hand.

"I'll take care of it."

"You sure?"

"I can wash dishes." He flashed that disarming smile again. "In fact, I do it pretty regularly."

One good quality didn't cancel out all the bad ones.

"Clay…about the job. I appreciate the offer, but I have to say no."

"Why?"

She shifted Jamie to her other hip. "I need

something I can do from home. So Jamie doesn't have to be left with a sitter or in day care. He's had so many disruptions these last few weeks, one more is just too much."

"Day care?" Clay stood up as well and came out from behind the desk. "I thought you understood."

"Understood what?"

"You can bring Jamie with you to work." He gestured to the corner. "Put a playpen over there. One of those bouncy-chair things. I don't care. This isn't exactly a professional office."

She stared blankly at him. "I can bring Jamie to work with me?"

"I told you that, didn't I?"

If he had, she hadn't heard him.

Clay moved closer, and Jamie reached for him. "I'd like it if you brought him. That way, I get to see him even more."

Another attempt to control her, or was he just being thoughtful and considerate?

Sierra wished she knew. Maybe then making a decision wouldn't be so hard.

Chapter Six

"He's forcing you," Gavin insisted, "and he has no right!"

Sierra loved that her brother was sticking up for her. She'd half expected him to support Clay, considering how traditional Gavin could be in his thinking and his past experience with Cassie's mother. Because of his ex, Gavin had missed out on most of Cassie's childhood and wouldn't wish the same on any father.

But he was also Sierra's big brother and for him blood was thicker than water.

"I don't know if he's forcing her as much as sweetening the pot." Ethan sat back, taking a sip of his coffee. While he was also concerned for her and Jamie's welfare, he happened to be best friends with Clay and would try hard to see both sides.

Gavin glared at Ethan. "You sound like you think she should do it."

"I think she should consider it. She said herself she freaks out if she has to be apart from Jamie. Even for a few minutes."

"He has a point," Sierra's father agreed. The four of them sat around the kitchen table, the dirty dinner dishes still in the sink waiting to be washed.

"She shouldn't have to be apart from him." Gavin pushed to his feet.

Ethan, the more easygoing of the two, stacked his hands behind his head and stretched out his long legs. "With joint custody, she'd get Jamie half the time. But if she lived with Clay, she'd get him *all* the time."

"I wouldn't be living with him," Sierra was quick to add. "The casita is entirely separate from the house."

"It's still on his property," Gavin grumbled.

"Technically, yes." She questioned how much of his annoyance at Clay was for her sake and how much was left over from when Bud Duvall sold their family's land out from under them. She'd thought Clay and Gavin had settled their differences when they became business partners.

Maybe not.

She was glad the rest of the family had driven into Scottsdale for some last-minute wedding preparations—which is what her brothers should be doing, too. The big day was Saturday, and there was precious little time left to handle the hundred and one details still needing attention.

Sierra glanced around the kitchen, her heart bursting with love. No way was she going to let her suit with Clay interfere with what should be the happiest day of her brothers' lives. She and Clay would have to get along, simple as that.

The debate between Gavin and Ethan continued with Jamie interjecting his two cents every now and then. He perched on his grandfather's lap, banging his toy pony on the table. Little by little he was warming up to his grandfather, uncles, aunts-to-be and cousins, which pleased Sierra immensely.

"Da, da, ba, be." Jamie pushed the toy pony into his grandfather's face.

"Hey, there." Wayne grimaced and averted his head. "Isn't it past your bedtime yet?"

"Bath first," Sierra said.

"Clay always thinks he's right." Gavin clearly wasn't letting the subject drop.

"And you don't?" Ethan slanted a good-natured grin at his brother.

"Sierra's place is with her family, and Jamie's place is with his mother."

"A father has a right to his child. You should know that better than anyone."

That shut Gavin up. There was nothing he wouldn't do, no lengths he wouldn't go to, to keep Cassie with him.

Was he any different from Clay?

Was she any different from Cassie's mother?

"I think you should move into Clay's casita." Her father's announcement brought a sudden halt to his brother's heated discussion.

"Are you serious?" Gavin demanded.

"Yes. For just the reason Ethan brought up. You went through hell those years you were separated from Cassie. We all did. It wasn't fair to you, to Cassie, and it wouldn't be fair to Clay."

"I'm not taking Jamie and moving across country," Sierra interjected. "Wherever I live, Clay will… He'll have Jamie half the time." Her mouth went dry at the prospect.

"The boy needs stability," her father persisted. "He's gone from home to home, parent to parent. You think shuffling him back and forth between you and Clay is going to provide him that stability?"

"No." Sierra reached over and patted Jamie's smooth cheek. "Which is why I'd rather have full custody and for Clay to have only visitation. For a while. Until Jamie adjusts."

"He can adjust perfectly fine at Clay's place."

Sierra wasn't sure she could, however.

"And you'd get to take him to work. How many employers will let you do that?"

"Day care wouldn't be an issue if I found a job I could do from home."

"Right. You look into that yet?"

"Some."

"Find anything that isn't telephone sales?"

"It's a tough job market. Something good will come along eventually." Hopefully her meager savings would hold out till then.

"Don't you want Sierra and Jamie here with us?" Gavin demanded of their father.

"'Course I do. But Clay's place is practically within walking distance. Riding distance, for sure. I can see my grandson every day if I want." Wayne lightened his tone. "Clay deserves the chance to raise his son. Just like you deserved the chance to raise Cassie."

"I like Clay, don't get me wrong."

"Then what is it?"

"Seems like the Duvalls are always taking from us."

Sierra thought her father might react more strongly to Gavin's statement, but he didn't. "Clay isn't his father. He's a good man."

"What about Sierra?"

"She'll be fine," her father said confidently. "Done pretty well on her own since college."

He was wrong on two counts. She hadn't done well on her own, especially during her pregnancy. And as far as being fine, the dispute was taking a terrible toll on her and that would continue even after it was settled.

She covered her father's hand with hers. "I'll always need you."

"And we'll always be here for you, sweetie pie."

Why hadn't she come home when she first found out she was pregnant instead of closing herself off?

Because her family had hated Clay until

last fall when he and her brothers had reconciled after capturing Prince.

It still seemed strange to Sierra that he was treated the same as before Sierra's mother died—like a member of the family.

What would Louise Powell have wanted for her daughter and grandson if she were alive today?

Sierra didn't have to think twice. Her mother was as traditional as the rest of her family and believed a child's parents should be married. She'd insist Sierra move into Clay's casita on the chance the living arrangement would lead to a marriage proposal. And she'd have had Blythe's support. Sierra could just see the two women putting their matchmaking heads together.

Was her father also counting on Clay proposing? She wouldn't put it past him.

Jamie let out a whiny cry.

Sierra reached for him. "Sounds like one of us is getting tired."

"Can't he stay up a few more minutes?" Her father attempted to distract Jamie without success.

"I want to finish in the bathroom before Cassie and Isa get home." She was acutely aware of how big a disruption she and Jamie were to the girls' established routine. They'd been patient so far, but it was only bound to get worse.

"Whoa, there," Wayne said when a full-fledged cry erupted from Jamie's mouth.

"Sorry, Dad." Sierra stood and took Jamie, snuggling him close to her chest in an attempt to quiet him. "When he cries like this, he's reached the point of no return."

"I can give him a bath if you want," her father offered.

"What? And leave me with these two?" The look she sent her brothers said, *Talk about something other than Clay.*

They ignored her.

If she didn't dread more fallout, she'd tell them she'd mostly made up her mind hours ago. She'd just needed that last little push and to be reminded of what was most important. Jamie.

Tomorrow morning, first thing, she'd call Roberto and inform him of her decision. He could tell Clay; she didn't think she could handle it.

Clay hesitated just inside the door. The noisy bar and grill was packed for a Thursday night. Then again, when wasn't it? He didn't frequent the Saddle Up Saloon for the very reason he'd come here tonight.

His father.

Bud Duvall could be found on his favorite bar stool most evenings from six to nine. Later on Fridays and Saturdays. He didn't have a drinking problem, none that Clay knew about anyway. Bud typically nursed two draft beers for as long as he stayed, always leaving a generous tip in exchange for "rent" on the bar stool. He often joked about the Saddle Up being his second home.

An unfortunately true situation that was no one's fault but his own.

Clay searched the large room, his gaze skimming a sea of cowboy hats and teased hairdos. He spotted his father in his usual place, center of the bar and, when the band wasn't playing, center of attention. Flanked by his regular cronies, Bud acknowledged everyone who passed by with a howdy or a firm handshake or, in the case of the fairer sex, a wide grin and appreciative once-over.

Some things never changed.

Clay crossed to his father, weaving right and left to skirt tables. Bud didn't see Clay until he was standing directly in the older man's line of vision.

"Lookie here, fellows," Bud boomed, his friendly voice a contrast to his wary eyes. "See what the cat drug in."

His father's friends greeted him warmly.

"Hey, Clay."

"Been a while, hasn't it?"

"Luke. Artie." Clay nodded, smiled. "How you doing?"

They exchanged small talk for several minutes before Luke and Artie offered flimsily concocted excuses and left. They probably figured if Clay had sought out his father after years of sporadic contact, it was probably an important and private matter.

"Buy you a drink?" Bud offered when the bartender made a pass.

"Club soda."

The bartender left to fill Clay's order.

"Since when you quit drinking beer?" His father studied him curiously.

"I haven't. Just not in the mood tonight." He didn't want any alcohol, even one beer's worth, dulling his senses. "Can we talk?"

"Sure."

"Some place less loud and less crowded?"

His father shrugged. He didn't relish abandoning his bar stool for any reason, including talking to his estranged son. "I'm free tomorrow."

Clay ignored the sarcasm. "This is important, Dad."

"Whatever you say." Bud drained the last of his beer and heaved himself off the stool. The same height as Clay, he carried an extra thirty pounds, most of it in the form of a spare tire hanging over his belt buckle.

Clay remembered when his father had been lean and muscled and strong enough to wrestle a full-grown steer to the ground one-handed. In those days, the Duvalls' cattle operation had been in full swing, and Clay and his father toiled twenty-four hours straight if necessary.

Bud sold the cattle operation when Clay was twenty-two. Clay had used his share of the proceeds, a share he felt he'd rightfully earned, to purchase the land on which he eventually constructed his rodeo arena. When his father sold the Powells' land two years later, Clay refused to take even one dime, though Bud had tried to convince him. They'd spoken rarely since then, Clay unable to get past what he considered his father's betrayal of a sacred trust.

In the span of a single day, the Duvalls had

gone from being the Powells' dearest friends to being their hated enemies.

Was it any wonder Sierra had feared telling her family he was Jamie's father?

"There's an empty booth in the corner." Bud walked ahead of Clay.

Not exactly quiet, but the location was marginally more private. At least Clay wouldn't have to shout his personal business in order to be heard over the din. He and his father had already created quite a stir with the regulars.

They sat on opposite sides of the booth, the ancient cushioned seat beneath Clay giving in some places and lumpy in others.

"How's your mother?"

Bud's question didn't come out of the blue. He always asked after Blythe whenever he and Clay talked.

"She's good."

"Still liking her job at the title company?"

"Very much." Clay wasn't in the mood for pleasantries. "Dad, I have some news. Good news."

"You're not moving again?"

"No."

"Didn't think so." He scraped a knuckle along his neatly trimmed salt-and-pepper beard. "Heard you're doing well with the rodeo arena."

Clay almost asked his father to repeat himself. The remark was the closest Bud had come to praising Clay since the day he'd brought home the state bronc-riding championship. Not long after that, Clay had cursed Bud and told him he didn't care if they ever crossed paths again.

He thought of Jamie. If someone had suggested to Clay ten days ago that he was the father of a toddler son, he'd have laughed in their face. Now, he was seeking custody and eager to turn his life upside down in order to have Jamie and Sierra included in it.

"I'm doing well enough. Being the only privately owned rodeo arena in Mustang Valley helps." Clay took a sip of his club soda, his throat inexplicably dry. Why was he suddenly nervous to tell his father about Jamie? "Sierra Powell is back in Mustang Valley."

"Been a while." Bud flinched ever so slightly. Someone who didn't know him might not have noticed.

Another time, he'd have tried to analyze that flinch. Tonight, he didn't care. "She brought her son with her. *Our* son."

Bud's brows rose until they disappeared beneath the unruly hank of silver hair covering his forehead. "You and her have a son? Why didn't you tell me?"

"I just found out myself. His name is Jamie. He's fifteen months old."

Bud chuckled. "I can't believe she let you within ten feet of her, much less into her bed."

Delivered with a humorous tone and coming from a friend, the comment could have been taken as a joke. From Bud, it smacked of an insult, and Clay's fingers involuntarily clenched.

"The Powells and I have made our peace," he said.

"Not then, you hadn't. When did you two hook up? Before or after Jessica?"

After? Did his father actually think Clay had violated his marriage vows? "Before. When Jessica and I were on the outs."

He didn't and wouldn't tell his father how devastated he'd been over Jessica dumping him—again—and how good Sierra had made him feel.

"What are you going to do?" Bud asked.

"Take care of Jamie. Sierra, too. I've filed a custody suit."

"What do you mean by 'take care of'?"

Be the best father I can, like you used to

be, he almost said. "Provide financially and emotionally. Share the parenting with Sierra."

"Marry her?"

Clay thought carefully before answering. It wasn't as if the idea hadn't occurred to him. But having recently survived six months of a marriage made in hell, he wasn't ready or willing to take the plunge so soon.

"No, we're not getting married." Frankly, he doubted she'd accept even if he proposed.

"What's the matter with you?" Bud's voice rose loud enough to generate stares from nearby tables. "Didn't I raise you right?"

"You did," Clay answered evenly. "And I promise you my son will never go without."

"He deserves the Duvall name."

"He'll have it. My attorney is filing an amended birth certificate."

"That girl deserves your name, too."

"That girl?" Could his father not bring himself to say Sierra?

"Don't get smart with me."

A bar was hardly the place to engage his father in an argument, but Clay did it anyway. "How can you sit there and question whether you raised me right, when you stole six hundred acres out from under the Powells?"

"I did no such thing." Bud leaned forward, bringing his face closer to Clay's. "I gave them the money so Louise could have a heart transplant. A lot of money. It wasn't my fault she died. Or that Wayne lost interest in the ranch."

"You promised to give the Powells first chance to buy back the land."

"I did."

"That's a lie."

His father's face flushed a deep red. "I've done a lot of bad things that I'm not proud of, but lying isn't one of them."

"Wayne would have moved heaven and earth to keep his land."

"Maybe you don't know him as well as you think."

"What are you saying exactly?"

Some of the fight went out of his father, and he toyed absently with the happy-hour menu. "Wayne couldn't come up with the payment. Not even a partial payment. I extended the loan. Interest free. By then, he'd run their operation into the ground."

Clay reeled. He hadn't heard this version before. "Why are you only telling me now? Why hasn't Wayne said anything?"

"The man lost his wife. His business was hanging on by a thread. He wasn't about to

admit he'd failed, and I wasn't about to pub-
licly shame him."

"You should have gone to Gavin and Ethan.
Given them the chance to repay the loan."

"Wayne asked me not to."

"Couldn't you have waited one more year?"

For the first time, Bud Duvall looked
beaten and a decade older than his fifty-eight
years. "Shoot, I'd have waited twenty years.
A hundred years. Wayne was the best friend
I ever had."

"So why ruin him?"

"You weren't even twenty when your mom
and I split. There are just some things a kid
shouldn't have to know about his parents."

"I'm not a kid anymore, Dad."

"You aren't, that's a fact." Bud tossed the
happy-hour menu aside as if it irritated him.
"One day your mother told me she was unhappy. The next day, she packed up, moved
out and filed for divorce."

That was what Clay remembered, but he'd
always assumed there was more to the story.

"Did you sell the Powells' land to try to
get her back?"

"She tell you that?"

"No, I'm making a leap."

Bud chuckled mirthlessly. "Well, leap in

another direction, pal. She forced me to sell the land because it was the only way I could raise enough revenue to meet her demands. She insisted on her half of our marital assets and refused to wait, even when I begged her."

Chapter Seven

Clay aimed his truck in the direction of Scottsdale and his mother's townhouse. Activating his Bluetooth, he pressed the speed dial. The call went right to voice mail, and he remembered her mentioning something about going to the theater with a friend. She held season tickets to ASU Gammage, had purchased them soon after she and his father divorced, the Director's Club, with preferred seating, backstage tours and VIP-lounge access.

Had she bought the tickets with money from the divorce? The Powells' money?

The possibility made Clay's stomach churn.

For years he'd believed his father to be the bad guy. A traitor. A betrayer. According to his father, those descriptors belonged to his mother.

How screwed-up could one family be?

He drove to Powell Ranch instead of his mother's home. Ethan was probably in bed, or would be soon, which is where Clay should be. Like his friend, he had an early morning.

His mind, however, was racing too fast to let his body sleep. He needed to talk to someone, and Ethan, as his best friend, was that someone. He'd get Clay out of bed if circumstances were reversed.

Ethan's truck wasn't in sight when Clay rumbled slowly through the ranch and toward the converted apartment beside the stables. No lights came on in the main house, though the back-porch light shone for several seconds, then went off. Late-night visitors to the ranch weren't uncommon. People boarding their horses often came by at odd hours to administer medicine or change wound dressings, check on pregnant mares and, on really cold nights, ensure their horses were properly blanketed.

Parking in front of Ethan's apartment, Clay climbed the porch steps and knocked on the door. No one answered. He scanned the immediate area and noticed what he should have in the first place. Ethan's truck wasn't here. Clay was tempted to wait for Ethan. Naw, he was probably with Caitlin at her condo in Mustang Valley. That was where Clay would be staying if he was about to be married in a few days.

Married.

He could still hear his father asking him if he was going to do the right thing and give Sierra his name.

Clay tested the doorknob and found it locked. He couldn't even hide out till morning. About to turn around and go…he had no clue where…he heard the crunch of footsteps on hard ground.

"What are you doing here?"

He spun at the sound of Sierra's voice. She stood half in the shadows, half in the glow of a silver moon hanging high in the sky.

"Hey." Guilt ate at him—for what *both* his parents had done to her family. He swallowed before continuing. "I wanted to talk to Ethan."

"He's not here."

"So I see. What you are doing out so late?"

"One of us is having trouble sleeping." She stepped out of the shadows, and Clay saw that she was balancing Jamie on her hip. He had one fat fist shoved in his mouth and was making whiny, snuffling sounds.

"What's wrong?" Clay came off the porch, his worried glance taking in his son from ski-cap-bundled head to footed-pajama toe.

"He's teething. I was talking to an old friend from work earlier, and she suggested taking him outside. She said sometimes a change in scenery helps."

"With the pain?"

"It's more of a distraction tactic."

Clay could use one of those. Maybe he should stroll around the ranch, too. He liked that idea, but only if Sierra went with him.

"Hey, you okay?"

He caught her studying him. "Me? Yeah."

"You look upset."

He shoved his hands in his jacket pockets. "I am. A little. Had a talk with my dad tonight. Told him about Jamie."

"Is he mad?"

He heard the accusation in her voice. "Not at all."

Clay was the one who was mad. Even now, as he recalled the conversation at the Saddle

Up, he realized his father hadn't asked one thing about his grandson or—this hurt the worst—if he could see Jamie.

Then again, Clay and his father had gotten off track. Way off track. And Clay had abruptly stormed out.

Damn it, none of this made any sense. His mother wouldn't have forced his father to sell off the Powells' land. She loved them.

Jamie whimpered.

"Can I hold him?" Clay asked.

"Um, sure."

He'd anticipated an argument.

Jamie went willingly into Clay's arms and quieted almost immediately. "Got a sore tooth, pal?" He tucked Jamie's head into the crook of his neck and closed his eyes. Not everything in life had come easy. Love for his son did. Very easy. "I know how painful that is. Had some bum teeth myself a few years back."

"Wisdom teeth?" Sierra asked.

"Impacted wisdom teeth. They pulled all four, which explains why I'm not very wise."

She smiled at his lame joke, the most relaxed he'd seen her since she'd arrived home. With moonlight turning her hair the color of quicksilver, she looked prettier than ever.

The pull of attraction he'd felt earlier when they were touring the casita didn't just return with a vengeance. It hit him like a sledgehammer to the gut.

"I'm sorry you argued with your dad."

"It wasn't an argument as much as a heated discussion."

"About Jamie?" Her tone became defensive again.

"My mom. Their divorce. The sale of your land." Without thinking about it, Clay had started swaying slowly, and Jamie's eyes drifted closed. "Can I ask you a question?"

"Sure." Sierra reached out and stroked Jamie's back.

Clay stared at her hand, recalling when she'd similarly stoked his back, offering comfort when he'd been heartsick over losing Jessica. It was the first time he'd noticed Sierra as someone other than his best friend's little sister.

His body stirred, reacting to the memory.

They'd made a baby together. But they'd also shared more than simple physical intimacy. He'd opened his heart to her, and she to him. If only he'd been smarter, seen that he and Jessica weren't cut out for each other.

He probably shouldn't have had those wisdom teeth removed, impacted or not.

"What did your dad tell you when mine sold off your land?"

The corners of her mouth turned down. "Why do you ask?"

"Did he mention my dad giving him an opportunity to buy back the land before he sold it?"

Her gaze clouded in confusion, then darkened. "I'm sure your father didn't give him any opportunity whatsoever."

Clay took that as a no.

If, as his father claimed, Wayne Powell had the chance to repay the loan and keep his land, why not tell his children?

Would Clay? Honestly, no. He'd have too much pride to admit to his children he couldn't come up with the money.

Had he really been wrong about his father all these years? His father had said he was protecting Wayne. But at the expense of his relationship with his son? It didn't make sense, not to Clay.

"Why are you asking?"

He considered telling Sierra the specifics of his conversation with his father, then decided against it. His dad could be lying. Clay needed to talk to his mother first. Even then, Wayne should be the person to tell his children the truth.

"My father mentioned something I hadn't heard before."

"What something?"

"It's probably nothing." He gazed down at his son who was soundly sleeping in his arms. When had that happened?

Longing squeezed his heart. This, a child of his own, was what he'd wanted, what he'd almost had and lost.

Only he'd always imagined having a wife along with his child. A wife he loved to distraction.

His gaze shifted to Sierra, slightly rumpled and yet incredibly appealing. She might have been his wife if things had worked out differently.

"Want me to take him?" she whispered.

"I'll carry him to the house if that's okay."

"Sure." She gazed adoringly at Jamie.

Clay almost felt like a heel insisting on taking Jamie half the time.

Not enough to alter his stand, however. Then again, he might be more inclined if Sierra ever looked at him the way she did their son.

They walked in silence to the house, entering through the kitchen door. Expecting Sierra to take Jamie from him, he was surprised when she said, "Do you want to put him to bed?"

They tiptoed down the hall and to the guest bedroom. The entire household appeared to be retired for the evening. In the room, Sierra switched on the nightlight. A ceramic teddy bear in pajamas sitting astride a calico pony provided enough illumination for Clay to see the portable crib on the floor beside the bed.

Together, he and Sierra gently removed Jamie's outerwear. Clay lowered Jamie into the crib, laying him on his back. His limp arms fell to his sides, and his mouth moved noiselessly.

"Is he talking in his sleep?"

Sierra smiled fondly. "Babies do that." She laid his jacket on the chair beside the dresser. "Once he's down for the night, he usually doesn't wake up till morning."

"Is it always so hard to get him to sleep?"

"Not usually."

"You tired?" Clay only now observed the shadows beneath her eyes and the lack of color in her cheeks.

"Some. You, too?"

"It's been a tough week."

"Yeah, it has."

They stood for a moment, Clay thinking what it would be like to hold her in his arms and have her rest her cheek on his jacket as Jamie had done.

Talk about making a complicated situation more complicated.

"I should get going."

"I'll walk you to the door."

He knew every inch of the Powells' home, having spent endless hours there growing up. He could have found his way to the kitchen door with a triple blindfold.

Even so, he accepted Sierra's offer.

On the patio, he turned to bid her good-night.

She stood, nervously rubbing her palms on her pants.

"Something the matter?"

"I, um, was going to have my attorney contact you tomorrow."

"About the custody agreement?"

"Yes. And the living arrangements." She exhaled, clearly struggling with what to say.

She was turning him down.

Disappointment arrowed through him. Up

until this moment, he hadn't realized how much he wanted her and Jamie to live with him. Granted, in the beginning, it had been a ploy to be close to his son. But that had changed.

"Take another day or two before you say no. It would be good for Jamie to have—"

"I'm accepting your offer."

His jaw went slack. "You are?"

"And the job, too."

"Wow."

"If you still want me to work for you."

"I do." He grinned. Stupidly, he was certain. "That's great."

"There are going to be some conditions."

"Naturally." His grin widened. "I figured as much."

"I'll move in and start work once we've ironed out the agreement."

He grabbed her by the waist and hugged her fiercely. Sierra and Jamie were coming to live with him! "Thank you."

She let out a startled gasp but didn't withdraw.

"I'm really glad you said yes." He breathed her in. She smelled as good as he remembered.

"Me, too." She raised her arms, hesitated,

then slid them around his neck, returning his hug.

Yes, nice. Really nice.

Wait, no. He reminded himself this was a friendly hug between two people whose only concern was the well-being of their son.

His body had other ideas, as did his hands, which skimmed her back over the material of her too-bulky, too-thick sweater.

He couldn't stop himself. Her curves were too perfect, her scent too intoxicating, her skin like satin.

Her skin?

When had his hand moved to caress her cheek?

"Tell me no." He bent his head, his lips seeking hers.

She didn't. She couldn't, not with him kissing her.

Big, big mistake. Huge, like the size of an entire mountain range.

Exactly the kind of mistake that had gotten Sierra into trouble before.

She knew she should hightail it out of there as fast as her legs could carry her.

But she didn't move.

It wasn't Clay's arms circling her that prevented her escape. No, no. Or the sensation of his mouth, firm and warm and with just enough pressure to send a delicious thrill winding through her. A small part of her had wanted this kiss since she'd glimpsed him standing outside of her brother's apartment. Possibly since the first day she came home.

His lips moved over hers, nibbling, teasing, coaxing a response from her. He got it, all right.

She sighed and leaned into him, anticipating the moment when he'd deepen the kiss. Soothe the needy ache inside her.

Just when things started to really heat up, he abruptly withdrew. She almost lost her balance, and a startled sound escaped her.

A low groan escaped him. "I shouldn't have done that."

Yeah, and she shouldn't have turned into mush the instant their lips touched. What was wrong with her?

He studied her with a piercing stare that split her apart and, she was convinced, revealed every one of her secrets.

"Don't look at me like that. It was just a kiss."

"Right."

"Oh, please." She rolled her eyes. Clay

wasn't going to learn how much the kiss had affected her.

His satisfied grin infuriated her. She was half inclined to tell him she'd changed her mind about everything, the casita, the job, the custody agreement, then she instantly reconsidered.

The better course of action would be not to lose her head again. She could do that. Keep their relationship strictly professional and avoid him as much as possible.

"See you tomorrow night." His voice was low and slightly husky and reminded her of other kisses shared beneath shimmering moonlight.

"What time are you coming by?" she asked with a not-that-I-care demeanor.

"I figured we'd meet up at the rehearsal dinner."

Shoot, she'd forgotten about the dinner. Well, it couldn't be helped. She'd agreed to attend even though she wasn't officially a part of the ceremony. Both Sage and Caitlin had offered to make her a bridesmaid, but Sierra had declined, preferring to watch Jamie and assist with the reception.

"See you there."

His gaze glided over her, slow and hungry. "You don't have to walk me to my truck."

"I wasn't going to." Of all the nerve.

He lowered his head.

For one wild second, she thought he was going to kiss her again. Her body ignored the directives her brain screamed at her and slowly drifted toward him.

"Jamie's crying."

She was so distracted by Clay's breath caressing her neck, what he said made no sense. "Excuse me?"

"Jamie. He's awake."

She listened and heard faint crying coming from inside the house. It galvanized her. "I'd better go."

With a final glance at Clay, she scurried inside and to the bedroom, hoping the noise hadn't woken up the rest of the house.

Jamie stood in the portable crib, clinging to the side, tears spilling from his eyes and red splotches on his cheeks.

"Sorry, baby." She lifted him into her arms and pressed him to her, alternately bouncing him in her arms and swaying back and forth. The wailing continued. Worsened.

How long had he been carrying on before Clay heard him? Sierra couldn't believe she'd been so wrapped up in their kiss she'd ignored her child's cries.

Then again...

She shivered at the memory of Clay's lips parting hers.

This absolutely had to stop! Jamie was her first and only concern.

"Definitely, positively, that is never going to happen again," she vowed aloud.

Aware of the sudden quiet, she peered down at Jamie. He'd stopped his fussing, and his hazel eyes stared fixedly at her as if he didn't buy a single word she said.

"Who was here?" Sierra's father stood in the bedroom doorway.

"Clay." At the mention of his name, a warm flush crept up her neck to her face. "Did Jamie wake you with his crying?"

Or, had her father been up already and seen her and Clay kissing?

Please, no!

"I was reading."

Whew!

Her father came into the room and smiled fondly at Jamie, who was fighting sleep tooth and nail. "Kind of late for a visit. What did Clay want?"

"He was looking for Ethan."

"Like I said, kind of late."

"He was upset. I guess he saw Bud and told him about Jamie. They got into some kind of argument."

"About Jamie? Of all the—"

"It had more to do with Bud selling our land and his parents' divorce."

"For the love of God! Why are they still rehashing that?"

Sierra thought her father's outburst a bit much but dismissed it. Between the wedding and her return, everyone's emotions were running a little high.

"Clay asked me if Bud ever gave you an opportunity to buy back the land before he sold it."

"What did you tell him?" There was no mistaking the apprehension in her father's voice.

"That Bud didn't give you *any* opportunities."

"Good. Because he didn't."

"Well, whatever Bud told Clay must have been pretty upsetting for him to drive out here at this time of night."

"He'll say anything to get out of taking

responsibility for what he did to us. I hope Clay's smart enough not to be suckered in."

"I'm sure he is. Why else would the two of them have been at odds all these years?"

"If he wants to be part of this family, he'd better stay clear of Bud. I mean it."

Would her father really cut out his grandson's father from their lives?

"I think he's trying to mend broken bridges."

"No point in that."

"Really, Dad? Isn't that what *we're* doing?"

"It's different."

Sierra didn't agree. Bud Duvall had done a terrible thing to her family, but he'd also done one very kind and generous thing. He'd given them another fifteen months with her mother they wouldn't have had without the loan of his money for her heart-transplant surgery.

"I don't want Duvall coming to the wedding."

"He wouldn't dare. And Clay wouldn't dare invite him."

Her father grumbled to himself.

"Don't you think it's time to put the past to rest? For Jamie, and all your grandchildren."

Not that Sierra was ready to forgive Bud Duvall, but her own actions these last two years, her neglect of her family and their willingness to welcome her back with open arms, had given her a new perspective.

She might feel differently if her family was still on the brink of financial ruin instead of owning two thriving businesses, her brothers getting married and expanding their families.

"He took advantage of me at the lowest point in my life."

Sierra sighed softly. Continuing the discussion was useless. Her father harbored too much anger.

She lowered Jamie into the portable crib, and he went instantly to sleep. "This teething ordeal is awful."

"Ethan was the worst of you three."

"Seriously? He's always been so easygoing."

"Not when it came to teething or the terrible twos."

She followed her father to the door, glad to see him back to his old self. "I have something to tell you. I've decided to move into Clay's casita."

"Makes sense."

His underwhelming reaction wasn't what she'd expected, considering how adamantly he'd supported the idea over dinner earlier.

"I'm moving as soon as the joint-custody agreement is finalized."

"Why the wait?"

"There are still some details we have to agree on first. And, besides, I don't want to be moving in the middle of the wedding."

"It probably sounds strange, a father encouraging his unmarried daughter to live with a man."

"Not *with* him, Dad. In the casita." The difference was important to her.

"In the casita," he repeated and smiled. "Much as I'm going to miss you, you're making the right decision."

Was she? If not, it was going to be one very long year.

"Good night." She stood on tiptoes and kissed her father's cheek.

"Sleep tight, honey." He started to leave, then stopped in midstep. "Promise me something."

"What's that?"

"If Clay does reconcile with Bud, and he starts hanging around Clay's place, don't talk to him."

"You know I wouldn't."

"Okay. See you in the morning."

She shut the door behind him, concern stealing over her.

Why had her father felt the need to extract a promise from her?

More worryingly, why had he refused to meet her gaze while doing it?

Chapter Eight

Sierra sat in the front row, Jamie perched on her lap, the fingers of one hand dangling a newly purchased plush toy in front of him. The fingers of her other hand were tightly crossed and had been for the last thirty minutes.

Please, please, don't cry.

All through the ceremony, Jamie had behaved beautifully. That could change in an instant. She'd hate for his wails to disrupt what had turned out to be a simple yet charmingly perfect country wedding.

The brides and grooms were exchanging their vows in the front courtyard of the Powell family home. Boughs from the paloverde and desert willow trees stretched out like reaching arms, providing a natural arch beneath which the wedding party stood. A golden afternoon sun glowed warmly, prompting several of the men to shed their suit jackets.

Two hundred white metal chairs had been rented and arranged to face a stunning view of Mustang Valley, at the heart of which lay Mustang Village. It was a fitting backdrop for the wedding ceremony. Mustang Valley had once belonged to the Powells, and even though civilization had encroached in recent years, the land would always belong to them in spirit.

More accurately, to her father and brothers. Sierra was still searching for where she truly belonged. She'd lived two-thirds of her life in Mustang Valley, and yet San Francisco felt more like home to her. She missed it. Her friends, too, and her job and even her tiny apartment.

On Monday, two days from now, she and her son would be moving into Clay's casita. She had yet to ship her personal belongings and furniture from San Francisco, preferring to "wait and see." In fact, she, her father and Gavin had gotten into a disagreement about it yesterday morning. They wanted her to have everything shipped now, make her return to Arizona permanent. Sierra had resisted, causing the argument to end in a stalemate.

On Tuesday, she'd start working for Clay at the rodeo arena. Mostly, she was terrified. She was also excited. About the job, not the move.

Living in close proximity to Clay worried her. She hadn't been able to fully suppress the fluttering in her middle that had started with their kiss the other night. How much worse would it get when she was sharing meals with him and passing him in the hall on the way to the laundry room?

Shifting Jamie to her other knee, she observed Clay from her place next to her father.

The two best men, Clay and Conner, another childhood friend of her brothers', wore black jeans, black Stetsons and bright turquoise Western shirts. Despite the casualness of his clothes, Clay looked handsome and mouthwateringly sexy. So much so, Sierra had to force herself to gaze at the brides and grooms.

Both women had chosen traditional white gowns, minus long trains. Sage's was high-waisted in order to draw attention away from her pregnancy. Gavin and Ethan, gorgeous in their black Western-style suits, couldn't take their eyes off their respective brides.

Isa stood by her mother and Cassie stood by her father. The girls wore matching turquoise dresses. Isa clutched the basket that had contained rose petals. She'd taken her job as flower girl very seriously and remained absolutely still, as she'd been instructed to do all last week. Cassie was the one fidgeting. When asked if she'd wanted to be a second bridesmaid for Sage, she had refused, opting instead to be the ring bearer. Her father had agreed but only if Cassie wore a dress. It was a compromise. She definitely preferred denim to taffeta.

Sierra's emotions, already riding close to the surface on this special day, overflowed, and she dabbed at her tears. She had always dreamed of a wedding like this. Not the country theme as much as having family and friends gathered in one place to witness the joining of two hearts, together forever.

She felt an invisible tug and lifted her head to find Clay staring at her, his expression unreadable. And then, suddenly, it wasn't. She saw longing and desire and a need that pierced her with its intensity.

No, she must be mistaken. He didn't want her like that.

She glanced quickly away, shaken by the raw power of his gaze. When she turned back a moment later, his attention was on the minister, giving her reason to suspect she'd allowed her imagination to run amuck.

"Gentlemen," the minister boomed, his crinkly smile taking over his entire face, "you may kiss your brides."

That was all the encouragement her brothers needed. While Gavin cradled Sage's cheeks tenderly between his hands and brushed his lips across hers, Ethan bent Caitlin backward over his arm and planted a toe-curling kiss on her mouth. The guests broke into cheers and applause.

Sierra leaned down and rubbed her temple against Jamie's. "Uncle Gavin and Uncle Ethan just got married."

"May I present Mr. and Mrs. Gavin Powell and Mr. and Mrs. Ethan Powell."

More applause accompanied the minister's pronouncement. Jamie joined in, squawking and clapping his hands. The wedding procession began, and the couples left the courtyard to the music of an acoustic guitar. The best men and maids of honor followed in the wake of the brides and grooms.

Connor had been matched up with Sage's cousin, Clay with Caitlin's roommate from nursing school. The woman was strikingly beautiful, with wavy brunette hair that cascaded down her back. Sierra tried not to think of what an attractive couple she and Clay made. How the woman's slim arm linked possessively with his. About the two of them chatting up a storm at last night's rehearsal dinner.

"You ready?" Her father pushed to his feet, his eyes misty. He'd mentioned several times today how much he wished Sierra's mother was there.

She stood, holding on to Jamie, and the three of them went down the aisle after the brides' families.

"I'm going to the kitchen to see if I can help with the food." A popular Mexican restaurant had been hired to provide the catering.

"You can't," her dad said, dragging her and Jamie through the house. "We have pictures to take."

Outside, the wedding party gathered in the open area between the house and the stables. With three families involved, there were a lot of people. Someone had laid out a large green indoor/outdoor carpet where the photos would be taken. Rental chairs were brought over for those who wanted to sit.

One of the Powells' wranglers led over Prince, the wild mustang her brothers and Clay had captured. The horse took one look at the brides in their billowing dresses and balked, snorting loudly.

"What are they doing with Prince?" Sierra asked her neighbor.

It was Clay who answered. He was, she noticed, minus Caitlin's maid of honor. "Your brothers decided they wanted him in some of the photos."

"I don't think Prince is on board with the idea."

"You could be right."

They watched and waited from a safe distance while Gavin and Ethan tried to calm the horse. It was a slow process. Sierra regretted not grabbing one of the empty chairs.

She was acutely aware of Clay. His height. His breadth. The rugged strength beneath his polished exterior. His undeniable sex appeal.

"I get that Prince played a part in bringing Gavin and Ethan together with their wives, but this might be going a touch overboard."

"What can I say? Your brothers are hopeless romantics."

"*My* brothers?" She gaped at Clay. "You have got to be kidding."

They both laughed. Sierra stopped abruptly when she caught Ethan staring at them, a knowing smile on his face.

Jamie chose that moment to start fussing.

"Hush now, baby." She wiggled the plush toy in front of him. He'd been so good. If not for the pictures, she'd put him down for a nap.

"You want me to take him for a bit?" Clay offered.

"Do you mind?"

"Are you kidding?"

Her arms were getting tired, and maybe a change would perk Jamie up. Prince was finally cooperating, and the photographer, a pretty young woman, was hurriedly snapping shots of him, Sierra's brothers and the brides.

Jamie, as always, delighted in going to his father. He immediately grabbed at Clay's hat.

"Later, buddy. When we're done with the pictures."

Finally, the wrangler led Prince away, or was it the other way around? The photographer began calling out groupings. Clay, as best man, was in more shots than Sierra and

Jamie. The minutes dragged on and on. Soon, Jamie started crying and nothing Sierra attempted quieted him.

Just when she thought they were done and she could leave, Clay put an arm around her shoulder.

"Can you take one of the three of us?" he asked the photographer.

"Certainly."

"Jamie's tired," Sierra protested. "And crying."

"This won't take long," Clay insisted.

"Can we do it later?"

"The photographer is leaving."

"I'd love a picture with Jamie, too," Blythe said. "Maybe one with Wayne and I and Jamie."

"Good idea!" Clay agreed.

Sierra fumed. This was the side of Clay she liked the least. The pushy one.

Unable to refuse without making a scene, she allowed the photographer to take several shots of them in different poses. Jamie cried in every one. When Clay suggested a shot with all "the men"—him, Jamie, Sierra's brothers and father—she reached her boiling point.

"Clay, it's time for Jamie's nap."

"One more."

Was this a preview of what it would be like when she and Clay shared custody of Jamie?

She allowed one more photo. When it was over, she wrenched Jamie from Clay much as he'd done to her before, and started for the house.

"Sierra—"

"He needs a nap, I need a rest and they're getting ready to serve the food."

Clay started after her only to stop when someone called his name. Good. Hopefully, he got the message. He wasn't the only one in charge.

Was it too late to change her mind about the casita and the job?

Probably. She'd signed the custody agreement yesterday, along with the employment contract.

Escaping to her bedroom, she hastily changed Jamie and settled him in the portable crib, the plush toy beside him. Jamie protested loudly for about ninety seconds, then fell into an exhausted sleep.

Sierra sat on the edge of the bed, only to stand up again. She should be out there, mingling with guests, helping in the kitchen. Jamie would be fine without her. She really did hover excessively. Checking on him again, she stepped outside the room—and breathed. She was going to be okay. She couldn't leave the house without Jamie, but she could leave the room.

After visiting with a few old friends, she busied herself helping old Mrs. Ruesga serve up enchiladas and tamales while simultaneously protecting the three-tiered wedding cake from curious youngsters.

Cassie and Isa burst into the kitchen. "We're hungry," they said in unison.

The rest of the wedding party wasn't far behind. Clay came in last, Caitlin's maid of honor adhered to his side.

Hmm.

"Can I fix you a plate?" Sierra asked her brand-new sisters-in-law.

"I'm too excited to eat," Caitlin exclaimed.

"I'm not." Sage patted her stomach. "And don't be stingy."

After the initial rush of hungry guests slowed, Sierra and the other helpers began clearing tables.

"Cassie," she called. "Would you mind giving us a hand?"

"With what?" A hint of teenage attitude laced Cassie's voice.

"Take this empty garbage bag and go through the house, collecting trash."

Huffing impatiently, she grabbed the bag from Sierra.

"Did I say something to upset you?" She thought she got along well with her niece. She'd certainly made an effort since coming home.

"Nope." Cassie spun on her heels and left.

Sierra's first inclination was to do nothing. Cassie was probably in a mood brought on by all the excitement. Perhaps she was jealous of her new stepmother and all the attention Sage was getting.

On second thought, what kind of aunt would Sierra be if she didn't attempt to find out what was bothering the girl?

She went in search of Cassie and found her in the hall.

"Cassie, sweetie, what's wrong?"

She said nothing and dropped an empty plastic cup in the garbage bag.

"Come on. Talk to me."

To her surprise, Cassie whirled on her. "You're going to leave again."

"What gave you that idea?"

"I heard you yesterday morning with Grandpa and my dad. You won't have your junk shipped here because you're not sure you're staying."

"Sweetie, that's not the reason." Except it was. Somehow Cassie had figured out Sierra wasn't quite ready to put down roots.

"You hurt Grandpa. And my dad and Uncle Ethan, and you're going to do it again."

Cassie stormed off, leaving Sierra all alone to face the small gathering of stunned wedding guests.

"She doesn't mean it."

At the sound of Clay's voice behind her, Sierra cringed. Of all the people to witness her scene with Cassie, Clay had to be the one. "You heard?"

"Most of it."

Damn.

"Come on," he said.

Not waiting for an answer, he took her by the hand. She accompanied him reluctantly through the living room and outside to the front courtyard. It was nearly empty. Most of the guests were congregating inside or on the back patio where tables had been set up. Clay and Sierra sat in chairs near the make-shift altar, far enough away so no one could hear their conversation.

"Cassie's a good kid," he began.

"I know that."

"She's very protective of Gavin. Of their relationship. She resents her mother for running off to Connecticut and not letting her visit Gavin until last summer."

Sierra stiffened. Clay was lecturing her, and she didn't like it. "You and Cassie have a lot of long talks?"

"Me and Gavin. He's the one Cassie has the long talks with."

Of course they did. Sierra was instantly contrite. "I'm not like her mother."

Clay, thankfully, didn't state the obvious—which was that Sierra was exactly like Cassie's mother.

No wonder the girl was angry at her and didn't trust her.

There was a lot of that going around.

"If you give Cassie a chance," Clay continued, "you'll find a nice kid beneath that tomboy exterior."

"I like Cassie. And I'll talk to her. Tomorrow, when things aren't so hectic."

"Good. Now, about your furniture."

"Please, Clay. Not today."

"You're right. I guess I'm like Cassie, I don't want you to leave."

She gazed out at the valley below, remembering when she was Cassie's age and riding horses along the river with her brothers.

"I apologize for being prickly. Here and earlier during the photographs. I don't react too well to being pressured."

"Maybe that's something we can discuss during counseling."

She groaned. "Don't remind me."

They'd scheduled the first of their weekly sessions for this coming Wednesday.

"I admit, I can be a little pushy."

She wished his crooked smile wasn't so appealing. "A little?"

"What do you say we work with the counselor on our character defects?"

Against her will, she smiled. "There's still my dad and brothers. They're every bit as pushy as you."

"Afraid that's your problem to deal with."

She sighed. "Oh, joy."

"We're going to make this work, Sierra. You'll see."

He oozed confidence. She, on the other hand, wasn't sure about anything.

Meeting his gaze, she inhaled sharply. That same longing she'd seen on his face during the ceremony was back.

No man had ever looked at her like that before, unless she counted the night two years ago when she and Clay went from being friends to lovers in the span of a single heartbeat.

Suddenly nervous, she straightened. "I really should check on Jamie."

Clay didn't restrain her. Not physically. It was his eyes that cemented her in place, quickened her pulse, set her senses awhirl.

He raised his fingers to brush a strand of hair from her face.

Was he going to kiss her again?

Bad idea. They shouldn't.

She braced herself. Gave in. Gave up. What good would it do to fight the inevitable?

All at once, cool air struck her in the face. Clay had pulled back, was starting to rise.

Anger bloomed inside—at herself. What a fool she'd been. How often would he hurt her before she learned?

She stood so quickly her chair wobbled.

"Sierra, it's not—"

"Forget it."

"There you are!" Caitlin's maid of honor came up the aisle toward them, her sensual smile targeting Clay.

"Hey, Trista," Clay said.

Trista! That was the reason Clay hadn't kissed Sierra.

Relief filled her.

Relief that she'd been stopped in the nick of time from making another mistake. No other reason, she told herself.

"Sierra," Trista cooed. "I haven't had a chance to tell you how pretty you look. That dress really brings out the color in your cheeks."

Her dress? Hardly. Clay and their near-miss kiss was responsible.

"I came to tell you they're getting ready to pour the champagne and cut the cake. Clay, you have to make your toast."

"I'll join you shortly." Sierra exited the courtyard ahead of Clay and Trista, glad for an excuse to get away.

Smiling and saying hello to the guests she passed, she hastened to the bedroom. This was the longest she'd been away from Jamie, and she was proud of her progress.

Easing the door open, she stepped quietly inside the room and whispered, "Hey, handsome. You awake?"

She froze, staring at the empty portable crib. A strangled cry—her own—filled her ears.

Jamie was missing!

Oh, my God, oh, my God, oh, my God! Where was Jamie?

Terror assailed Sierra, shattering her composure, icing her blood. Grabbing at the sides of her head, she whirled, frantically scouring every corner of the room on the chance he'd managed to escape the crib and toddled off. Ripping the quilt aside, she fell to her knees and looked under the bed.

Nothing!

The closet was also empty.

Someone had taken him. *Stolen* him! Right out from his crib.

She tried to breathe but her lungs had collapsed. What was she thinking? She should never have left him alone for even a second.

Bolting from the room, she ran straight into Clay.

He grabbed her by the shoulders and steadied her. "Are you all right? I thought I heard something."

"Jamie's missing!"

"Missing?"

"He's not in his crib." She began to blubber. "I put him down for his nap, and now someone's taken him."

"Calm down, honey."

"I can't." She tried to shake free of his

grasp. "I have to find him. Before something happens."

"You look inside, I'll look outside."

His calm demeanor outraged her. Did he always have to be in such freakin' control?

"No! I'll look outside." Sierra couldn't explain it, but she was convinced whoever had Jamie had fled the house and was already driving off.

Flinging aside Clay's hand, she tore through the house and out the kitchen door.

Clay called after her.

She ignored him. There were so many people. Hundreds, all of them talking and drinking and mingling on the patio. How easy it would be for someone to hide Jamie inside a coat or jacket and stroll nonchalantly away with him.

"Careful now, slow down," a man warned.

"Did you lose something?"

Yes, her son.

It occurred to her to stop and inform the guests of what was happening rather than plowing over them in her haste. Possibly enlist their aid. That would take too much time, however. The kidnapper was getting farther and farther away with each second.

Cars were everywhere. In the parking area

behind the barn. Beside the stables. Next to the house. Her heart pounded inside her chest, hard enough to fracture her ribs. Where to start looking?

She heard an engine roar to life and ran in that direction. The heel of her shoe caught in a pothole, causing her to stumble. Regaining her balance, she surged ahead. Whoever had Jamie, they were not leaving this ranch. If necessary, she'd plant herself directly in their path and not move.

Then she saw it, a vehicle pulling out from behind the mare motel!

"Stop, stop," she hollered.

The vehicle came into view. Not a passenger car but a tractor with a feed wagon hooked to it. One of the ranch hands was getting ready to hay the horses.

She ground to a halt and blinked, her vision clouded from perspiration—or was it tears?

She was too late. Jamie was gone. Taken from her again.

The ground beneath her feet seemed to shift as if disrupted by tremors. A wave of dizziness left her faint and disoriented.

"Sierra!" Someone called to her from what sounded like a great distance away. "Sierra!"

She answered, except her voice came out a strangled sob.

What should she do?

Call the police. Yes, right away. Before too much time passed. And obtain a list of the guests from her family.

"Sierra!" The voice drew closer.

Fighting another debilitating wave of dizziness, she tried to bring the figure sprinting toward her into focus. It was Clay, and he was wearing an enormous smile.

A smile! There was only one reason for it.

Her knees collapsed.

"We found him." He caught her as the last of her strength deserted her. "He's in the house."

"Thank God," she said and burst into tears.

He wrapped his arm around her waist, and she leaned heavily on him, appreciating his strength. They walked her back to the house. Sierra would have preferred to run but her bones had yet to solidify.

"Where was he?" she asked feebly.

"My mother has him."

"Your mother! Why?"

"I don't know. I didn't ask. I was just so glad to find him."

Well, Sierra was going to ask. And Blythe

had better have a damn good reason for putting Sierra through hell.

She and Clay went directly to the living room. Blythe sat in a wingback chair, Jamie on her lap. Several people—strangers, all of them—surrounded her and bent over Jamie, speaking to him in baby talk. He fussed and writhed and made unhappy faces. While getting better, he was still leery of people he didn't know.

Sierra broke away from Clay. The second Jamie saw her, he opened his arms to her. "Ma, ma, ma."

Her throat closed. This was the first time he'd called her Mama. He must have been just as scared as she was.

"Hi." Blythe greeted her warmly. "I hope you don't mind—"

Sierra lifted Jamie off Blythe's lap and clutched him to her chest. She wouldn't let him out of her sight ever again, no matter what.

"How could you take him and not tell me?" she demanded, her voice cracking.

Blythe's jaw dropped. "I'm…sorry. I didn't think—"

"Obviously, you didn't." Sierra stroked Jamie's back, as much to reassure him as herself.

"Sierra," Clay said. "It's okay."

"No, it isn't. She had no right to take him."

Twin spots of color appeared on Blythe's cheeks. "I meant no harm," she said stiffly. "I just peeked in your room to show Lil and Beverly how cute he is, and he was awake, standing up in the crib. I brought him out here. I didn't think you'd mind."

"I do mind. Very much."

The half dozen pairs of eyes that had been fastened on Blythe switched to Sierra. She could feel the disapproval, the silent consensus that she was making a huge deal out of nothing.

She probably shouldn't have snapped at Blythe in front of her friends. But Blythe shouldn't have taken Jamie from his crib without telling Sierra.

"I apologize for losing my temper," she said. "I was upset to find Jamie gone."

"All you had to do, my dear, was look around."

Sierra bristled at Blythe's condescending tone. "I did look around. I didn't find him."

"Perhaps I should go give my respects to the brides and grooms." Blythe rose from the chair, tall and slim and dignified.

In comparison, Sierra felt small, and not just in stature.

"Mom, wait." Clay reached for his mother, then said to Sierra, "This is just a misunderstanding. Let's not blow it out of proportion. Not today. Jamie's safe. No harm, no foul."

A misunderstanding? Sierra thought it was more than that.

Clay was right, however, about her brothers' wedding not being the time or place to discuss it. She would take the matter up later with him, and he could talk privately to his mother.

"Excuse me, please." Blythe slid past Clay, a thin smile on her face.

"It's all right," one of her friends soothed while casting Sierra an accusatory glance. "I'll come with you."

Fine, blame her. Sierra didn't care.

Okay, she did care. She didn't want her family's friends thinking badly of her.

"Mom," Clay said, his voice low but firm. "Sierra has a right to be upset. Don't be angry with her."

Blythe halted. "I'm not angry."

"Maybe *angry* isn't the word."

"She overreacted. I'm the boy's grandmother. Can't I pick up my own grandson from his crib when he's awake?"

"No one is saying you can't pick up Jamie."

The look Clay gave Sierra was kind, not condoning. "She's been through a lot lately. More than you know. And if you did know, you wouldn't think she overreacted."

He was defending her. Taking her side. In front of his mother and her friends.

Gratitude vanquished the last of her anger, and she smiled at him.

He pinched Jamie's cheek. "Do you think this little guy's old enough for some wedding cake?"

"Plenty old enough."

She turned, intending to make amends with Blythe, only she and her friends were gone, and a heavy silence had descended over the room.

Terrific. Sierra had gone and spoiled her brothers' wedding.

Chapter Nine

Sierra answered the phone, a smile in her voice. "Good afternoon, Duvall Rodeo Arena. How may I help you?"

Clay sat in a visitor chair observing her at work, his open laptop computer balanced on his knees. Her first day on the job and already she sounded as if she'd been at it for months.

"Yes, I can get that for you. Hold on a second." She opened a three-ring binder containing the rodeo arena's rates and policies. "Are you interested in just bull-riding or also bronc-riding?"

Clay returned his attention to the monthly financial reports on the laptop screen, keeping one ear tuned to Sierra's conversation. They'd spent an hour when she first arrived at the office going over the types of calls she could expect and how to respond. Clearly, Sierra was a fast learner and not bragging when she'd referred to herself as the "go-to" assistant at her former job.

She'd spent the majority of yesterday moving into the casita and rearranging it to suit her tastes. He'd wanted to be more involved, his curiosity admittedly piqued. It was her father's help she'd enlisted, not Clay's, so he had yet to see the changes she'd made.

Frankly, he couldn't care less. He was just pleased that she and Jamie were here.

As if detecting his thoughts, his son banged his toy pony on the side of the playpen.

"Ba, da, da."

Clay put a finger to his lips. "Hush, son. Your mommy's on the phone," he said softly.

Jamie grinned, displaying yet another new tooth.

They'd set the recently purchased playpen up in the corner. Sierra had protested, not at the location but that Clay had refused to let her pay for it. He'd also purchased a full-size crib for the casita. In hindsight, he should have taken Sierra with him to the store. But then they probably wouldn't have agreed on which was the best brand. He and Sierra did have a tendency to take opposite sides of every issue.

Except for his mother removing Jamie from his crib during the wedding reception. His mother had been wrong, and he fully intended to discuss the subject with her when she came by in a little while to join him, Sierra and Jamie for dinner.

It had required almost no coercion on his part to convince both women to accept his invitation, and Clay was glad they seemed eager to make amends.

Before dinner, however, he needed to have a different discussion with his mother, this one about what his father had told him at the Saddle Up Saloon. Between kissing Sierra and the wedding, he'd gotten understandably sidetracked.

Jamie's banging escalated, and he emitted a loud shriek.

Sierra grimaced, though her tone remained pleasant. "Thank you for calling," she told the potential customer. "We'll see you tomorrow morning." Hanging up the phone, she sighed. "Baby, you have to be quiet."

Jamie grabbed the side of the playpen and rattled it.

"I think he's getting a little tired of being cooped up," Clay said.

"Yeah." She eyed Jamie worriedly, her thoughts clear. Their son was only going to get bigger and louder.

"Give him a chance," Clay said. "He'll settle down. Get used to the routine."

She didn't reply, merely got up from her chair and gave Jamie a toddler biscuit.

Clay hoped she'd eventually be agreeable to day care or a sitter, the sooner, the better. Her anxieties would be debilitating, for her and Jamie and Clay, too. He was counting on the counseling sessions to make a difference.

Sierra had been upset when she'd first learned she couldn't bring Jamie with them into the sessions and parenting classes and had almost backed out. Whatever argument her attorney had employed had had a positive effect. She'd consented to having Wayne accompany them to watch Jamie in the waiting area.

It was a step, and Clay was proud of her. When he'd told her so yesterday, she'd blushed. Very prettily, he might add.

He closed his laptop and got to his feet, purposefully distracting himself. This wasn't the first time he'd thought of Sierra as more than just the mother of his child. It wasn't even the first time today. He needed to get a grip on himself, and fast, before she sensed the change in him, panicked and moved out when she'd only just moved in.

That girl deserves your name, too.

Clay swallowed, his father's words ringing in his ears.

He wanted nothing more than to be the best dad in the world to Jamie. He *would* be the best dad. Did that require he marry Sierra? He found her attractive, desired her, thought there couldn't be a more caring and devoted mother for his son. But he wasn't ready to walk down the aisle with her. Not until he'd fully healed from the wounds Jessica had inflicted.

His gaze went to Jamie, his heart swelling with love. How could Jessica have been relieved to lose their baby?

How could Sierra have given theirs up?

"I'm heading outside," he told her, wanting to clear his head. "Conner's delivering some of the mustangs from Sage's sanctuary, and then Mom will be here. Will you be okay flying solo?"

"As long as Jamie's quiet. He's usually napping by now. I think he finds the office too interesting."

"I like that he's taking an interest in the business."

Sierra laughed.

Clay didn't. If she decided to stay more than the three months they'd agreed to, this could truly be a family business.

He bent and kissed Jamie on the top of the head on his way out the door.

In the main arena, several pairs of team ropers were practicing, reminding Clay he should have Sierra confirm the herd of weanling calves scheduled to arrive this week. Also, check on the rental contract for the three bulls and seven bucking horses they would be sending to the Helzapoppin Rodeo in Buckeye next month. Batteries Included, his best bucking horse, had already earned enough money to support the rodeo arena through May. At this rate, the large gelding could easily qualify for the National Finals Rodeo in December.

He'd be Clay's first stock animal to qualify for a world championship event and could potentially bring in a slew of new contracts.

Not bad for being in business less than two years. If things kept on the way they were, Clay really would have something of value to leave to his children.

Children? As in plural?

He'd always envisioned himself with two or three. The head of a large, boisterous family. Being an only child, he'd missed having brothers and sisters. That was probably one of the reasons he'd been so close to Ethan and Gavin and had considered Powell Ranch his second home.

His son deserved siblings.

What if Sierra met someone and got married? What if she and her husband had children?

Clay didn't like that idea. He'd marry Sierra himself first, whether he was over Jessica or not.

He slowed his steps, slowed his racing thoughts.

Better to hold off, see how this co-parenting arrangement progressed. He'd married once in haste and entered into an affair in haste. Each time, someone had walked away hurt. He wouldn't make the same mistake a third time.

* * *

Ten minutes later, Clay rounded the corner of the main horse barn and spotted Conner's truck and trailer. His friend and fellow best man was at that moment unloading a pair of feral mustangs, one bay, one buckskin.

"Need some help?" Clay hollered, quickening his steps.

"Sure do. These two boys have yet to learn any manners." Conner opened the rear gate on the trailer. "Watch out!" he yelled a scant second before the buckskin kicked.

Clay ducked, the lightning-fast hoof missing him by inches. "I see what you mean."

Once out of the trailer, the horses behaved marginally better. They allowed Clay and Conner to lead them to a small pasture behind the main horse barn and well away from the other livestock.

Conner opened the gate. "Ethan sure has his work cut out for him when he and Caitlin return from that resort in Sedona."

Gavin and Sage were also on their honeymoon—at a five-star hotel in Palm Springs. Clay got a kick out of imagining his rough and rugged buddies in the lap of sophisticated luxury. Then again, they were newlyweds and were probably staying in their rooms till noon. Clay would if it were him.

He and Conner walked the young geldings along the pasture perimeter, acquainting them with the fenceline before removing their halters. Immediately, the horses galloped in circles, bucking and rearing playfully before investigating the feed and water troughs.

"They *are* a bit ornery," Clay agreed.

He and Ethan had decided before the wedding to bring these two horses to Clay's place as a first step in moving the mustang sanctuary from Powell Ranch. When Gavin and Ethan returned, they'd transport the rest of the horses and continue training.

"How 'bout you and me head to the Saddle Up for a beer and burgers?" Conner asked on the walk back to his truck. "My treat."

"Can't. Mom will be here any minute. She's having dinner with Sierra and I."

"Another one bites the dust," Conner grumbled.

"Why don't you come by this weekend? We'll grill some steaks and watch the basketball game."

"You sure Sierra will let you off your leash?"

"It's not like that," Clay insisted as his friend climbed in behind the wheel.

"Yeah, right." Conner started the engine. "See you Sunday." He slammed the door shut and, with a wave, drove off, the empty trailer making a clanging racket as it bumped over the rough ground.

Was it like that?

Things had definitely changed these last few weeks. Before Sierra came home with Jamie, Clay would have gone out with his friend in a heartbeat. Now, he had chicken and vegetables in the slow cooker and was trying to remember if he'd put out clean towels in the hall bathroom.

Wasn't all that different from being married.

Except he didn't get to wake up next to Sierra every morning.

A memory surfaced, one where he *had* woken up next to her at the Phoenix Inn. She'd been naked, save for a tangled sheet covering her shapely form. Her mussed hair had fallen appealingly over her sleepy eyes, and her tanned skin glowed from their long hours of lovemaking.

She'd never looked prettier or sexier.

He could think of worse things than waking up beside her every morning.

His cell phone rang. Nothing like the sight of his mother's number on his caller ID to banish all inappropriate thoughts of Sierra.

"Hey, Mom."

"I'm running a bit behind," she informed him.

"No problem. See you soon."

Clay conferred with his barn manager on the way to the house. He tried not to dwell on dinner. Just because Sierra and his mother had agreed to come didn't guarantee the evening would go smoothly. His mother pulled up just as he reached the driveway.

"Where's Sierra and Jamie?" she asked, kissing his cheek and handing him an apple pie to carry in.

"At the office."

"How's she doing?"

"Great. She's catching on really fast."

"No, I meant how's she doing after...the wedding?"

"She hasn't mentioned you once, if that's what you're wondering."

"It is." Blythe sighed wistfully. "I'm hoping she and I can put all that unpleasantness behind us."

"Me, too."

They made their way inside where Clay put the pie on the kitchen counter and checked on the chicken.

"How soon till she's finished work?"

He added water to the slow cooker. "About an hour."

"Do you have to rush back to the office or can we visit?"

"Actually, I was planning on you and I visiting." He attempted to keep his tone light.

His mother saw right through him. "What's wrong?"

Clay propped his back against the kitchen counter. "I spoke to Dad last week."

"Did you?" Blythe sat at the table. "You know I've always hated that you and he were estranged."

"No, Mom, I don't. I can't remember you ever telling me anything like that."

She hesitated, as if carefully considering her answer before responding. "That was a long time ago. I've moved on. I'm glad to see you're doing the same thing."

"My conversation with Dad was far from amiable."

"Oh, dear."

Clay crossed his arms. "He mentioned something. About you. Something that was news to me."

Her eyes grew wary. "What was that?"

"He said he sold the Powells' land because you forced him to. That you wanted your share of the marital assets and wouldn't wait. The only way he could come up with the money was to exercise the clause in his loan contract with Wayne."

She stared fixedly at her clasped hands. "He said that, huh?"

Clay's stomach dropped to his knees. It was true. He could read it in her expression. "How could you?"

"I didn't force him to sell the land. What assets he liquidated was his choice."

"What other assets were there to liquidate? He'd already sold the cattle operation." And given Clay half the proceeds, which he'd gladly accepted.

If only he'd realized his parents would be divorcing a few months later he'd have refused the proceeds in order to save the Powells' land. By then, however, he'd already purchased the property for the rodeo arena.

"I had no clue what other assets," Blythe

said testily. "Your father handled all our finances. He told me only what he thought I needed to know."

She was right about that.

"But you did insist on your share in the divorce settlement."

"I honestly thought your father still had his share of the money from selling the cattle operation."

"What happened to it?"

She shrugged. "Between the time we drafted the property settlement and the divorce was finalized, he invested the money in stocks. The bottom fell out of the market, and he lost a considerable sum. He didn't tell me about it. Too ashamed, I guess."

Like Wayne had been too ashamed to tell his kids about his financial mishandlings.

"I'm sure your dad thought Wayne would make his payments. I assumed he was doing so all along. Certainly no one anticipated he'd sink into such a deep and lingering depression after Louise died."

Wayne's children had obviously thought the same thing as his mother had, and Wayne didn't correct them.

Clay rubbed the back of his neck. What a

mess. And the ones who'd suffered the most were Sierra and her brothers.

"I was sick when I learned about the land sale. I loved Louise like a sister."

"Only sick? Weren't you the least bit guilty?"

"I barely slept for weeks. If I'd had any indication Wayne had defaulted on the loan and your father was selling the land, I'd have told him not to."

"You let me blame Dad all these years for something that wasn't entirely his fault."

Blythe squeezed her eyes shut. "I did, and I regret that."

"Why?"

"Divorce is complicated. I was furious with him. It skewed my thinking."

"Tell me about it. Been there, done that." Clay ground his teeth together. "I agree Dad can be a jerk sometimes. Tough. Strict. Uncompromising." He might have disagreed with his dad while he was growing up and rebelled more than once, but he'd always respected his dad until he'd sold the Powells' land. "But it's not like he gambled or lied to you or cheated on you."

"He didn't." His mother sighed. "He also wasn't entirely responsible for our marriage ending. It's taken me a while, but I see where I contributed. Greatly," she added, in a wobbly voice.

Clay wanted to vent more but he could see she was truly broken up.

"What are you going to do?" she asked.

"I'm not sure yet. Talk to Dad."

Tomorrow. After he'd had time to sort through everything.

This conversation would be considerably less heated and involve considerably more forgiveness.

"I can't tell you how sorry I am," Clay's mother said. "I was thoughtless and selfish. I should have sent someone to find you and let you know I had Jamie. Better yet, I should have found you and asked you myself if it was okay. Next time, I will. I promise."

"Thank you." Sierra smiled. "And I'm so sorry I snapped at you."

Clay watched his mother and Sierra make their sincere and heartfelt apologies to each other.

"Are we good then?"

"Yes, we're good." Sierra reached over and took Blythe's hand.

The three of them sat at the kitchen table,

having recently finished Clay's chicken dinner. Jamie occupied his high chair, strategically placed next to Sierra. He evidently loved cooked carrots—smashing them into a pulp as much as eating them.

Everyone, including Jamie, was amused, until he started flinging carrot pieces onto the floor. Then, only Oreo was amused. The old dog lapped up the carrots with the dexterity and speed of an anteater.

"Enough of that," Sierra said and replaced the carrots with a sippy cup of milk.

Jamie immediately shared his milk with Oreo by tipping the cup over and spilling several drops on the floor.

"No, baby." She righted the cup. "Don't give any milk to the dog."

Jamie banged the tray and babbled as if to say, But he's hungry.

Oreo concurred and gazed at Sierra with soulful eyes.

"Honestly." She huffed. "Between the two of you, I'm going to have to break out the industrial-strength cleaner."

"Don't worry about it," Clay assured her.

"Nonsense. You cooked dinner, I'll wash up."

"Why don't we both wash up?"

"And why don't I watch Jamie in the family room while you do?" Blythe offered.

Clay waited for Sierra to say no. After her scare at the wedding, he doubted she'd leave Jamie alone.

"That would be great. And maybe you can give him a bath, too."

Blythe's hand fluttered her heart. "I'd love nothing better."

Sierra turned to Clay. "Is it all right if we use your bathroom?"

He cleared his throat, which had tightened during the last several seconds. "Have at it."

Over thick slices of apple pie, Blythe regaled them with stories of when Clay was Jamie's age, how cute he'd been and some of his more adventurous baby pranks. Normally Clay would have put an end to the torture. Instead, he let her talk uninterrupted. Sierra—where she got the patience Clay had no clue—listened raptly.

Jamie tossed several apple chunks to Oreo.

Sierra administered stern looks to boy and dog. "What am I going to do with you?"

Clay chuckled, only to be silenced by a sobering thought. He was having dinner with his family. How long had he wished for this very thing? A sense of amazement and profound satisfaction enveloped him.

It faded the next instant.

If Sierra decided she hated living here, took a job elsewhere, they'd be back to square one in three months.

Regardless what she did, wherever she went, he would not lose Jamie. He might be a brand-new father, but he loved his son more than life itself.

While Clay carried dishes to the sink, his mother filled the tub in the hall bathroom, and Sierra made a quick trip to the casita. She returned with a armful of bath paraphernalia. A towel, toys, three bottles, one of them shampoo, a hairbrush, a toothbrush, pajamas and some kind of ring contraption with suction cups on the bottom.

"This bathing stuff is kind of involved," he said as she traipsed through the kitchen.

"You have no idea."

After five minutes, he began to suspect Sierra wasn't able to leave his mother alone with Jamie after all. Well, next time. It was enough that she and his mother had resolved their differences.

He began loading the dishwasher.

Partway through, Sierra joined him. "That was a disaster."

Clay hid his pleasure. "What happened?"

"Jamie decided he needed a prewash in the toilet."

He grimaced. "I'm not going to ask."

"You're smart not to."

"I'm curious, what's that ring contraption?"

"To stabilize Jamie so he doesn't slip on the porcelain. He sits inside it."

"I guess our moms lived on the edge."

She laughed, a sound Clay liked to hear. "I admit, some of the baby safety gadgets these days are a little extreme. But most of them are clever and really useful."

They made quick work of the remaining dishes. When they were done, Clay fed Oreo. Dog food, not carrots and milk and apple chunks.

"I'm going to check on Jamie," Sierra said breezily.

Clay was impressed she'd gone as long as she had without dashing to the bathroom.

"While you do that, I'm going to take Oreo outside. He likes to go on a stroll every evening around the back pasture. His one shot at exercise."

"Wait a minute, and I'll go with you."

What?

Hell, yes.

He would, he realized, wait a very long time if necessary.

Chapter Ten

Clay retrieved his jacket from the hall closet and Sierra's old sweater from the back of the kitchen chair where she'd left it.

"Thanks." She tugged the bulky garment over her head, then freed her hair from the neck hole. The long sleeves hung past her wrists and the hem nearly to her knees.

Clay thought she looked pixieish and rather cute.

Like the time she'd worn an old work shirt of his with nothing underneath but a teeny-tiny pair of pink panties.

They'd spent a lazy Saturday afternoon lounging on his couch, eating popcorn and watching movies. By the middle of the second movie, she wasn't wearing anything at all, and his hands were caressing her silky bare skin.

A rush of desire plowed through him with the force of an avalanche.

"All set?" His fingers fumbled with the zipper on his jacket.

She rolled up her sweater sleeves. "I noticed earlier it's cold outside tonight."

Good. Bring it on. Cold evening air was just what he needed right now.

Oreo ambled slowly along behind them as they walked from the house toward the pastures. The pair of feral mustangs delivered earlier that day whinnied and ran over to the fence, snorting lustily as Clay and Sierra approached.

"We don't have to go very far," he said. "Oreo's not as frisky as he once was."

"He looks like he's doing okay. And so am I. You don't have to fret."

"I'm not." He was too busy entertaining inappropriate thoughts about Sierra to fret, or do anything else for that matter.

She checked her watch. "I have about fifteen minutes. That seems to be my threshold before I start going ballistic."

Was she ever going to let him live that down?

"You'll get better."

"I want to get better. I hate being this afraid. It's not healthy for either me or Jamie."

"The counselor will teach you how to cope."

"Among other things, I hope."

"Like what?"

"How to effectively communicate and negotiate." She slanted him an amused smile. "How to stand up to pushy people. How to conquer my insecurities."

What about them and their relationship? Clay was starting to think his goals were evolving from co-parenting Jamie with Sierra to co-habiting with her to—

Best stop there. He wasn't ready for what came next.

"You made my mother very happy tonight. You didn't have to let her bathe Jamie."

"I like your mother."

"She likes you, too." Where was a snake or bat when you needed one? Anything to spook Sierra and cause her to jump into his arms. "I'm going to invite my dad over this week to meet Jamie."

Sierra went abruptly quiet.

It killed his ardor better than the cold air.

He probably should have waited to tell her

but he didn't dare risk her finding his dad at the house.

"He's Jamie's grandfather," Clay explained. "I want them to meet."

"I thought you and he didn't get along."

"We haven't been. I'd like that to change."

"Why now?"

He couldn't tell her his mother had allowed him to unfairly blame his father for years, not without dragging Sierra's father into the discussion.

"What if I said no?"

"I would try and convince you otherwise."

"And if I still said no?"

"Grandparent visitations are covered in the custody agreement. Monthly supervised visits."

"So, we're going by the agreement verbatim?"

"It's why we drew it up," he said reasonably. "So we wouldn't have these arguments."

"We're not arguing, Clay."

Not yet, but the mood had certainly shifted—downward. "Have you asked your dad about mine lately?"

He sensed more than saw her withdrawal.

"The other night, when you came by."

The night they'd kissed.

"I told him you'd seen your dad earlier at the Saddle Up."

"How did he react?"

"Is it important?"

"I'm just curious to know if he's any less angry."

She chuckled mirthlessly. "He's not. In fact, he warned me to stay away from your dad."

Clay would give anything to know the reason why. Was Wayne afraid Clay's dad would give away his biggest secret? Or were his parents distorting the truth in order to make themselves appear better?

"We should get back." Sierra stopped and peered anxiously over her shoulder. She'd apparently reached her threshold.

Clay reversed direction. "Oreo's getting tired anyway."

"Can I ask you a personal question?"

"Fire away." He'd asked one of her. She deserved the same.

"Why did you and Jessica divorce?"

That came out of the blue.

Then again, maybe not. Sierra was living with him, more or less. She was naturally curious about his ex-wife, as he was curious about the men in her past.

"I think the better question is why we married in the first place."

"You were in love."

"Not the healthy, happy kind of love. Not the kind that sustains two people for a lifetime."

"Lust?"

"There was that, I won't lie." He paused, waited for Oreo to catch up with them. "Jessica infatuated me from the moment I met her. And she knew just how to work that infatuation to her advantage. She always held back a little, enough to keep me on the hook. She'd break up with me then take me back with no rhyme or reason other than her own unpredictable whims."

"It was a game to her."

"Not entirely. That was just how she operated. I'm not sure she was even conscious of it."

"Didn't you get fed up with her manipulations?"

"I did. And when that happened, she'd pile on the charm. Next thing, I'd be suckered in all over again."

"What prompted the divorce?"

"She didn't want children. Not right away and possibly not ever."

"Isn't that something you decided on before you got married?"

"I talked about having kids all the time and failed to notice her lack of enthusiasm. My mistake was assuming the absence of a no meant yes. Shortly after we married, she got pregnant."

"She did?" Sierra let out a soft gasp.

Clay had told only his mother and a few close friends about the baby. It was too hard on him, too many sad memories.

Not, he noticed, with Sierra. The pressure in his chest wasn't there, and he could breathe without experiencing a sharp, stabbing pain.

It had been the same two years ago when he'd poured out his heart to her after his and Jessica's latest breakup.

"I was thrilled. Jessica wasn't. I figured she was simply scared about being a first-time mother."

"What happened?" Sierra asked, her voice low and strained.

She must have realized that she and Jessica were pregnant at the same time, Sierra further along by a few months.

"She miscarried. At fifteen weeks."

"Oh, Clay. How tragic." Sierra touched his arm, let her fingers remain.

"It was rough. I was disappointed."

Disappointed and devastated and guilty. He could still hear the doctor gently advising them it wasn't their fault the fetus hadn't thrived.

How could the baby not thrive when he'd already loved him or her so much?

"Jessica, on the other hand, was relieved. She went right out and changed her birth-control method to something more reliable. Didn't bother telling me. I had to accidentally discover her stash of pills."

"Nothing is worse than losing a child." Sierra stared at the ground in front of them.

"For some of us." He covered the hand she'd rested on his arm. "If I overreacted when I first learned Jamie was mine, I apologize. I had a knee-jerk reaction."

"I'm glad you told me. It explains a lot."

"I did tell you because I want you to know how serious I am about being a good father and making this arrangement of ours succeed."

"I am, too."

She met his gaze boldly, and, for the first time, Clay believed her.

"Somebody's tired." Clay's mother cuddled with Jamie on the family-room sofa. All the lights were dimmed and soft music played from the sound system's built-in speakers.

Clay tarried behind while Sierra went over and peered down at grandmother and grandson, her features radiant.

"It's almost his bedtime."

Jamie lay with his head in the crook of Clay's mother's arm, sucking his thumb, his eyelids drooping heavily. Oreo lumbered over to the rug at their feet and dropped onto it with an exhausted sigh.

"Looks like it's someone else's bedtime, too." Clay grinned. He himself was too wired to sleep after his conversation with Sierra.

Sierra held out her arms to Blythe. "I'll take him and put him to bed."

"So soon?" The corners of his mother's mouth fell. She brightened almost immediately. "Thank you again for this evening. It's been wonderful."

"Anytime."

Did she mean it? Clay hoped so.

His mother stood and carefully passed Jamie to Sierra. "I think he's getting used to me."

The baby immediately wrapped his arms around Sierra's neck and snuggled his face in her sweater. She kissed the top of his head.

Jamie might be getting used to Clay's mother but he loved Sierra more than anyone.

She turned to Clay. "I'll see you in the morning."

He wasn't ready for the evening to end. "Can I go with you?"

"What about your mother?"

"Don't let me keep you, I have to leave anyway." Clay's mother went to the long breakfast bar separating the kitchen from the family room and retrieved her purse. "I'm scheduled to be at the office early for a big real-estate closing."

Sierra could still say no to Clay's request, manufacture an excuse. Lucky for him, she didn't, though her hesitancy left something to be desired.

"Good night, my dear." His mother dispensed hugs to Clay and Sierra, then tenderly kissed Jamie's forehead.

"I'll walk you to your car, Mom."

"Don't bother. Go put your son to bed."

She showed herself out.

"Come on," Clay said to Sierra when they were alone.

"There's all the bath stuff."

"Leave it till the morning." Better yet, leave

it and let Clay give Jamie his bath tomorrow night.

"Wait a sec. I'll be right back."

Before Clay had a chance to react, Sierra pushed Jamie at him. He took the sleeping boy and held him as he'd seen Sierra do. "Hey there, buddy."

Jamie protested grumpily but quickly drifted off, resting his cheek on Clay's chest.

Protectiveness and possessiveness welled inside him. This was his son, and Clay would do anything, give everything he had, to safeguard him.

"I love you, Jamie." He nuzzled the boy's downy hair. Hearing a noise, he looked up to see Sierra, her arms loaded with bath items. She stared openly at him.

"Is everything okay?"

"Yeah. Fine."

She appeared more rattled than fine.

Clay grabbed an afghan from the couch and draped it over Jamie to ward off the night chill. His son slept through the entire walk to the casita. Inside, Clay noted the changes. An old quilt on the bed. Clothes hanging in the closet. A floor lamp where there had been none.

The crib he'd purchased was no longer barren. Sierra had added colorful bedding, a mobile with shooting stars and quarter moons and an entire zoo's worth of stuffed toys.

"Is there room in there for him?" Clay asked.

She shoved some of the toys aside. "Now there is."

"Should we change him first?" Clay wasn't sure how often a baby needed changing, but it seemed like a lot.

"I think he's okay for now."

"Still sleeping through the night?"

"He didn't last night. I'm sure he will again as soon we get settled per—" She cut herself off.

What was she going to say? Permanently?

Clay liked her near slip.

He laid Jamie in the crib, stroked his back. "Sleep tight, buddy."

Feeling Sierra's gaze on him, he turned his head and met her bottomless blue eyes.

"I'm sorry," she said in a broken whisper.

"For what?"

"Not telling you about Jamie. I was wrong."

She'd admitted as much before but not with such genuine emotion. "Can you forgive me?"

"I already have. Jamie, the two of us raising him, is what's really important."

Every cell in Clay's body urged him to kiss

her. She was close enough, all he had to do was tilt his head, lean in.

Every cell in his brain warned him not to give in to his impulses. He and Sierra were making progress. She'd moved into the casita. Started working for him. Agreed to counseling sessions. Let his mother watch Jamie for a full fifteen minutes. Voluntarily handed Jamie over to Clay. He'd be a fool ten times over to screw it up by making an unwanted advance.

He took a step back from the crib. Before he could take a second step, Sierra reached for the collar of his jacket and pulled him toward her as she stood on her tiptoes.

"Sierra?" Her name came out a breath against her lush lips. Instantly, he plummeted, falling into her softness.

God help him, he never wanted to leave.

Her tongue touched his, and it was all over. Clay gave up resisting and kissed her with the voracity of a starved man. She responded, moaning low, setting every nerve in his body on fire. The control he thought he had snapped, and he threaded his fingers through the strands of her silky hair.

She came to her senses first and broke off the kiss.

"What was that for?" He had yet to release her, might never release her.

"I'm not sure," she said shyly. "It just felt right."

He couldn't agree more.

In fact, everything about her was feeling right as rain.

Even the idea of marrying her didn't scare the pants off him anymore.

Ten forty-seven a.m.

"How is the living arrangement working? Are you comfortable in Clay's casita?"

"It's very nice." Sierra smiled tightly.

Dr. Brewster, the counselor her attorney had recommended, waited patiently for Sierra to elaborate.

So did Clay. He sat beside her on the couch, tapping his foot.

"Nice as in the quarters are attractive?" Dr. Brewster had one of those open, pleasant faces that inspired confidence. "Nice as in you like being close to Clay and sharing parenting duties?"

Ten forty-eight.

Sierra wrung her hands. How was Jamie doing? Was he giving her father any trouble?

She'd been to the reception area twice to check briefly on them.

They were fine. Managing well enough, other than the magazine Jamie had torn to shreds.

Still, she couldn't shake the intense agitation that gripped her with vice-like tenacity.

She started to rise. "I'll be right back."

"Can you possibly wait?" Dr. Brewster asked. "We only have a few more minutes before the session's over."

Sierra didn't want to wait. She really didn't want to be here at all. But a deal was a deal.

Who knew it would be so difficult?

"Okay. I'll wait." She perched on the edge of the couch cushion and checked her watch again.

Still ten forty-eight?

She shook her wrist. Maybe her batteries were dead.

"About the living arrangement..." Dr. Brewster prompted.

"The casita is charming. Quite comfortable."

"And what about residing so close to Clay? How does that make you feel?" Dr. Brewster had asked the same question six times regarding six different topics.

Sierra had yet to meet anyone so concerned with how she felt.

"It's a little early to tell. This is only our third day." Sierra strained to hear through the closed door.

Silence. No crying, no screaming. No shattering of glass or the crash of bookcases toppling.

Had her father left with Jamie? Taken him on a stroll around the building? He wouldn't do that, would he? He'd promised to stay in the reception area until Sierra and Clay were done.

Ten forty-nine.

This session was never going to end.

"Well, *so far,* how's it going?" Dr. Brewster's question disrupted Sierra's thoughts.

"Okay."

"Just okay?"

Clay hadn't had any trouble when it was his turn to talk. He'd spent the first half of their session rambling on and on about how much he enjoyed being a father, how great it was having Jamie in his life, his plans for the future, blah, blah, blah.

Not that Sierra didn't think all that was wonderful. She just couldn't open up to a complete stranger as he could.

"Are you two growing closer?"

Sierra's knee jerked.

Clay raised his brows as if to say, *Tell her.*

She was not mentioning their kiss. Kisses, plural. Dr. Brewster would probably ask Sierra how she felt about them.

How did she feel?

Like she'd been lost forever and finally come home.

Wouldn't Dr. Brewster have a field day with that?

Sierra shouldn't have kissed Clay. The first one was kind of, sort of, understandable. He'd been excited that she'd agreed to move into the casita and accepted his job offer.

The second one? No excuses.

His story about Jessica's miscarriage and his tender confession of love for Jamie had moved her. As a result, she'd let down her guard. Boy, had she let it down.

What if he hurt her again?

He wasn't the same man she'd had an affair with two years ago, but he wasn't that different, either. She couldn't take a second devastating loss. And there would be no hiding from her family this time.

Ten-fifty.

"We're getting along better," Sierra hedged, "if that's what you're asking."

"Tell me more."

Dr. Brewster's second-favorite phrase.

"We were able to discuss Clay letting his father meet Jamie without screaming and shouting at each other."

"Very good. I'm impressed."

And not long after that, I kissed him.

She was growing closer to Clay, all right, in every sense of the word. The power of their connection, the depth of their attraction, scared her. She didn't like feeling vulnerable.

There, Dr. Brewster. What do you think of that?

"It's interesting you say you didn't scream and shout because I sense tension between you two."

"There's bound to be some tension," Clay said. "Just like any couple."

They were a couple now?

He covered Sierra's hands with his.

It was the first time he'd touched her since their kiss, other than to take her elbow as they were crossing the parking lot into the building. That touch had sent a tingle soaring through her. This one sent a wave of pleasure.

She had to force herself not to curl her own fingers around his.

Dr. Brewster glanced at their joined hands and jotted a note on her pad.

Great.

Ten fifty-one.

Sierra began rocking nervously.

"I'd like to make a suggestion," Dr. Brewster said. "Some homework for you to do between now and your next session."

"What kind of homework?" Clay leaned forward.

Sierra sat back, a sinking sensation in her middle.

"I know you mentioned that the two of you are having dinner together every night. And that you've done some activities with Jamie, like taking him on walks and putting him to bed."

And standing beside his crib, kissing.

Clay sent her a not so discreet glance. Was he thinking the same thing?

"What I'd also like is for you to practice some trust-building exercises."

Could trust be built with exercises? Sierra thought it had to be earned.

"For starters," Dr. Brewster said, "when you go on those walks with Jamie, I want you to tell the other person a quality or trait about them you appreciate and admire. Stick to those that relate to raising your son. Maybe, Clay, you admire Sierra's devotion to Jamie and maybe, Sierra, you admire Clay's protectiveness. Don't bring up anything negative and steer clear of your personal relationship."

That didn't sound entirely awful.

"Next, I want you to practice eye contact. It will help you be more comfortable with each other, more relaxed. Once a day, perhaps after your dinner together, you sit and stare into each other's eyes for a full sixty seconds."

Was she joking? If Sierra stared into Clay's eyes for sixty seconds, she'd wind up locking lips with him.

"No glasses or sunglasses and no squinting." Dr. Brewster smiled expectantly.

"Sounds okay to me."

Clay *would* agree.

"Do I have a choice?" Sierra asked.

"Of course," Dr. Brewster answered. "No one is going to force you to do anything you don't want to. I'd like you to consider the exercises, however. You might be surprised at the results."

Ten fifty-three.

Two more minutes and Sierra could leave.

The sound of a muffled chime sounded from the other side of the door.

Sierra stiffened. "What was that?"

"My eleven o'clock appointment arriving, I imagine."

Another patient. Of course.

Dr. Brewster took out her calendar. "Next Wednesday at the same time?" She looked to Clay and Sierra for confirmation.

"Sure," Clay answered for them both, already entering the appointment into his smart phone.

Hurray! It was over. Sierra sprang to her feet.

"And what about you, Sierra? What day works best for your individual session?"

Ah, yes. The individual sessions. Another agreement she'd made. More torture for her while Jamie and her father waited in the reception area.

"Mornings are best," she said. "I work in the afternoons."

"Friday at nine?"

She nodded.

"See you then."

Sierra raced to the door. Flinging it open, she burst into the reception area.

Her father stood at the window, Jamie beside him, busily leaving fingerprints all over the sparkling-clean glass.

"How was he?" Her heart didn't stop hammering until she'd lifted Jamie into her arms, inhaled his baby scent.

"Pretty good. He might have mutinied without those animal crackers you left me."

No one said much on the drive back to Mustang Valley. Clay dropped Sierra's dad off at the ranch, then drove home. She planned to feed Jamie lunch before heading to the office. Work would be a welcome distraction after the counseling session.

"See you at one?" she asked when Clay pulled into the driveway. He was going to show her the accounting software this afternoon.

"More like one-thirty. I have an appointment with the photographer from the wedding."

"Okay." Sierra thought that was strange but didn't ask. When it came to work, she was determined to maintain a strictly professional relationship with Clay.

"I'll bring her by the office when we're done touring the arena and barn since you'll be the one coordinating with her."

"I will?" Now she was really curious.

"She volunteered to take pictures of the feral mustangs for the sanctuary's newsletter and website. We're hoping professionally taken shots showing the horses at their best will generate interest and promote adoptions."

"What a great idea."

Clay lifted Jamie out of the car seat. "I think so, too. She and I talked about it at the wedding."

When was that? In between his conversations with Caitlin's maid of honor?

Sierra forgot about the photographer once she and Jamie returned to the casita. Feeding him lunch, freshening her makeup for the office and trying not to think about trust exercises occupied most of her thoughts.

In the office, she settled Jamie in his playpen. The morning's trip must have tuckered him out for, after only a few minutes of quiet play, he fell asleep.

Sierra checked the voice mail and email messages, responding to those she could and saving the others for Clay to handle. She was opening and sorting the daily mail when he brought the photographer into the office.

Sierra had forgotten how pretty the young woman was. Today, her highlighted hair was caught up in a high ponytail, and her brown eyes sparkled, especially when they lighted on Clay.

"Sierra, this is Dallas Sorrenson."

"Nice to meet you again." Sierra shook her hand.

"Same here. I'm really excited about this project and can't wait to get started. Animal causes are kind of my passion. I've also done photographs for several no-kill animal shelters."

They talked in subdued voices so as not to disturb Jamie.

"Are you a horse person?" Sierra asked.

"I was. Until college. Then, unfortunately, I had to sell my mare. Not enough money for board bills and tuition." She showered Clay with a gorgeous smile. "Clay says he'll take me riding."

"He did?" For some reason, Sierra's voice had risen half an octave.

"And let me watch one of the bull-riding practices next week. I love anything to do with rodeos."

She was sweet. Very sweet.

Sierra watched through the office window as Clay escorted Dallas to her car.

What was wrong with her? She wasn't the jealous type. And yet, here she was, spying on

Clay, fuming because Caitlin's maid of honor had fawned over him at the wedding and he'd shown the photographer around the arena.

Maybe she should ask Dr. Brewster about it in her individual session on Friday. No, that would be too humiliating.

Big whoop. Sierra and Clay had kissed. Twice. That didn't mean there was anything between them.

She was about to leave the window when Dallas and Clay suddenly hugged. A second later, she slid into her car, and Clay shut her door.

What the—! Did he hug all his business associates?

When he came into the office, a smile splitting his handsome face, Sierra met him in front of her desk and did as Dr. Brewster suggested, staring into his eyes for a full sixty seconds.

Just what she thought. She didn't trust him any more after the exercise than she had before.

Chapter Eleven

Clay craned his neck in an effort to see over the block wall to the casita. Nothing. Sierra still hadn't emerged from inside.

Did she have a case of cold feet? Had she allowed her anger to win out?

Frankly, he'd been a little surprised that she'd agreed to let his father meet Jamie today. When he'd initially broached the subject a couple of weeks ago, she'd been resistant.

Perhaps the counseling sessions they'd been attending were responsible. The positive effects were evident in other areas. Sierra was now able to leave Jamie with either Wayne or Clay's mother for a full hour with only mild anxiety. She and Clay were mostly on the same page regarding Jamie's upbringing. And the trust exercises—Dr. Brewster had added two more—were beginning to eradicate the barriers between them, enabling them to develop a sincere respect for each other.

Clay wasn't so optimistic he didn't anticipate setbacks. Like today, for instance.

He paced back and forth beside his truck, repeatedly checking the time on his smart phone. If they didn't leave soon, they'd be late for the picnic.

A Sunday afternoon at the park had been chosen for Jamie's first get-together with his other grandfather. Neutral territory, kid-friendly activities and plenty of other people providing a buffer. Sierra would feel less pressured, or so Clay hoped.

Dr. Brewster supported the meeting and the location. She believed Sierra and Jamie would benefit greatly from the experience.

Had Sierra changed her mind?

Or maybe something was wrong with Jamie. Forget pressuring her or being too controlling—her major complaint about him to Dr. Brewster—he was going to the casita to find out what the hold-up was.

He didn't get far. The side gate opened, and

Sierra emerged, Jamie in one arm, an over-flowing diaper bag in the other.

Relieved, Clay rushed toward her. "Here, let me help."

"Sorry I took so long. Jamie wasn't cooperating."

They added her diaper bag to the assortment of picnic stuff crammed in the truck's back seat.

"Should I bring the stroller?" she asked once Jamie was situated in his car seat.

"Probably."

She hurried back to get it.

Clay watched her, noticing her jeans and sweatshirt were far more "countrified" than her usual attire. It was a style that looked good on her. Almost as good as the little black dress and heels she'd worn to dinner the night they'd spent at the Phoenix Inn.

He winked at Jamie. "Your mama sure is pretty."

"Ma, ma, ma."

"That's right."

Sierra reappeared and, after loading the stroller in the truck bed beside the three folding lawn chairs, they left for the park.

She alternated between yapping a mile a minute and long stretches of silence.

"Are you nervous?" he asked.

"Some."

"We don't have to stay long."

"Will you mind greatly if I don't join in too much?"

"Naw. I'm just pleased you're going."

Clay had considered and reconsidered telling Sierra about his conversations with his father and mother, that his father had given Wayne ample opportunity to repay the loan. Ultimately, he'd decided against it.

He didn't know everything that had happened between his parents and Wayne. As the old saying went, there was more than one side to every story. If Clay interfered, Sierra might wind up angry at him, too, not just at his dad. It was a risk he wasn't willing to take.

He'd casually suggested on several occasions that she speak to Wayne about what had happened. For Jamie's sake. She'd refused. Her last reply was "Why rehash a past we can't change?"

That sounded more like Wayne than Sierra.

The only way they'd ever discover the whole truth, once and for all, was to approach Wayne, and Clay wasn't about to do that. Not when Sierra had finally consented to Jamie meeting his father.

She was staring out the window, gnawing on her lower lip.

"Dallas came up with a good idea the other day."

"Dallas?" Her head snapped around. "She was at the arena?"

"No, she called." Was it his imagination or did Sierra's eyes narrow? "I mentioned we were brainstorming fundraisers for the wild-mustang adoption."

The event was scheduled for next month. Sierra had been toiling diligently, often long into the evenings after Jamie went to bed. Ethan and Gavin had planned a demonstration to show how well-trained the mustangs were and their suitableness as Western pleasure mounts. Cassie was riding one of the older, gentler geldings. Dallas had volunteered to take pictures.

"She suggested we sell photos with Prince, charge people a nominal fee."

"I'm not sure about that." Sierra scowled. "Remember the wedding? Prince spooks easily."

"Dallas suggested we practice with him."

"Huh."

"He's a local celebrity. It's a good idea. I'd like you to coordinate with her on it."

"Whatever you say, boss. You're in charge."

Clay let the remark slide, attributing her surliness to nerves.

The entrance to the park came into view. Sierra offered no more than a murmured comment or two while they unloaded Jamie and the picnic supplies, which took an absurdly long time.

Clay surveyed the enormous pile. "I could use a third arm about now." His attempt at levity was ignored. "Sierra, you okay?"

"Don't worry about me." Her weak smile barely lifted the corners of her mouth.

How could he not worry? This meeting was important to him. She was important, too.

"Why don't we come up with a safe word? If things get too much for you, just say, 'Jamie's tired,' and we'll cut the visit short."

"You'd do that?"

"After all you've done for me? You bet."

She stared at him, as she did when they were practicing their trust exercises but not exactly. It was as if she wanted to see *him,* the real person inside, wasn't merely going along with Dr. Brewster's homework assignment.

Clay had been waiting weeks for just this moment.

* * *

Jamie sat in the middle of the blanket, picking raisins off the lint-ridden material and popping them into his mouth.

Sierra clasped her hands behind her back rather than whisk him away. She kept assuring herself babies didn't get sick and die from eating raisins off old blankets.

Bud Duvall, who also sat on the blanket, inched closer to Jamie. "Are those tasty?"

The boy glanced up from his task but didn't smile back at his grandfather. The older man's exuberance faltered briefly before he shored it up.

"It takes him a while to warm up to people," she said, then almost bit her tongue.

They'd been at the park half an hour, during which they'd laid out the blanket, set up the chairs and unpacked the food. This was the first Sierra had spoken to Bud.

"Well, that's just fine," he said, "because I'm in no hurry to leave."

Sierra was, but she had to admit Bud was being cordial and considerate. Not the least bit annoying or overbearing, which was what she'd feared. He was, she almost hated to admit it, the man she remembered from her childhood. Her father's closest friend. The husband of her mother's best friend.

How could that be? How could a considerate man practically destroy her family's lives and livelihood?

"He's teething," Clay explained. Like Sierra, he occupied one of the lawn chairs. "Makes him a little fussy."

"I had a root canal a few weeks ago. Hurt like a son of b— Like a son of a buck." Bud hooked a finger on his lower lip and tugged, showing Jamie his bottom teeth. "Right there," he muttered.

Jamie gawked at him with hugely round eyes, then burst into giggles.

"You like that?" Bud pulled the other side of his lip down.

Jamie shoved his own fingers into his mouth.

Bud chuckled and pinched his chin.

If Sierra didn't dislike the man, she'd have been enamored by the charming exchange.

"Anyone want a sandwich?" Clay popped the lid on the ice chest. "I have ham and Swiss, and peanut butter and bananas."

Peanut butter and bananas? Her guilty-pleasure favorite.

He'd remembered.

She'd made them for him one day when they'd driven to Saguaro Lake to watch the sunset. They'd taken the sandwiches with them and strolled the lakeshore until they found a solitary spot. Such a simple date and a simple meal. Yet it had been the most romantic day of her life.

"I'll try one of the ham and Swiss." Bud pushed to his feet with a grunt and sat in the empty lawn chair.

Clay rambled on about the wild-mustang adoption while they ate.

"That's a worthy cause, son." Bud dusted crumbs off his lap. "It does my heart good to know there's mustangs in the valley again, even if they aren't running wild."

"Did you ever see wild mustangs here?" Sierra asked.

"I did," Bud said. "I was just a boy. Nine or ten. The mustangs had all but disappeared before I was born. The tales my dad would tell…" He smiled, more to himself. "A small herd of horses made their way into the valley one winter from the mountains. They were skin and bones, and sick to boot. Didn't put up much of a fight when we rounded them up. There was a yearling, his dam, another mare and a stallion. Never saw horses that abhorred captivity more. They refused to eat and almost died."

"My dad saved them," Clay said.

"I don't know if I saved them exactly. I'd mix up a bucket of warm mash and feed the yearling by hand. The poor critter was timid as a church mouse but, eventually, he friendlied up and started eating. After that, the other horses did, too. Turned into some of the best horses we ever owned."

"What happened to the yearling?" Sierra asked.

"I kept him. Rode him nearly every day for the next twenty-six years, then retired him. Damn horse survived to be almost thirty. I must have covered a million miles of mountains and valley on his back. Speaking of teeth, his were so bad at the end and he grew so frail, I was back to feeding him warm mash by hand. I buried him at the trailhead behind the back pasture."

Sierra sat, transfixed. By the recounting and by Bud. His love of the land and the animals sang in his voice. She could see him as a young boy and an adult, patiently tending his beloved horse.

How could he have sold off her family's land? It didn't make sense.

"I'm sorry, Sierra. You must hate me, and I deserve it."

She drew back. Were her thoughts that apparent?

"Dad, you don't have to—"

"I do. Not a day goes by I don't think how different things might be if I'd told that investor no."

"Why didn't you?"

Sierra's question hung between them.

"At the time, I didn't believe I had a choice."

It wasn't much of an answer, but it was evidently the only one Sierra was going to get.

Bud stood, gathered up their trash and disposed of it in a nearby barrel. "You think Jamie would like to play in the sandbox?"

"I don't know." Clay turned to Sierra. "Do you think he's tired?"

Their safe phrase. All she had to do was agree with him, and, they could leave.

She started to say yes, but the desperation in Bud's expression halted her, caused her to reconsider.

"No," she told Clay. "I think he's okay for now."

For the second time that day, Clay craned his neck, seeking a glimpse of Sierra. To-

night, he was in the great room, staring out
the French doors at the casita. A light shone
in the front window, an indication she hadn't
gone to bed yet despite the lateness of the
hour. After almost three weeks of living with
him—*at his place,* he corrected himself—
he'd learned her habits. Sierra was early to
bed, early to rise.

Should he check on her? What if Jamie
was teething or coming down with a bug?
The next instant, he changed his mind. She
wouldn't appreciate him knocking on her
door at nearly eleven o'clock, even if his in-
tentions were good.

Were they good?

Clay had wanted to talk to Sierra since
they'd left the park. She'd been somber and
distant on the ride home and unresponsive
when he'd queried her.

They'd parted in the driveway, and he left
her alone the rest of the day. It had been an
emotionally draining afternoon for all of
them. And, for Clay, deeply satisfying.

Yet, instead of sleeping, he was pacing the
floor and borderline stalking Sierra.

Enough was enough. He had a full day
tomorrow. Some of the bucking stock were
returning from the Parada del Sol rodeo in

Scottsdale, the feed bins had to be cleaned in preparation for Monday's grain delivery and he had a conference call from a rodeo promoter out of Salt Lake City.

Clay was about to head to his room when the door to the casita opened. Sierra stepped outside, the exterior light bathing her in a hazy yellow glow. She wore scruffy slippers on her feet and a blanket wrapped around her like a cape. She went to the wrought-iron chairs in front of the kiva fireplace and plunked down.

Even at a distance, Clay could see her movements were slow and weighted, her shoulders slumped in exhaustion.

Clearly, Jamie wasn't teething or sick. Sierra wouldn't have left his side.

Perhaps she also had insomnia.

Stalker-like or not, he watched, unable to tear his gaze away from her. She opened the front of the blanket, revealing Jamie in her arms. A faint cry carried across the yard.

Clay didn't think twice before he fetched his jacket. At the door, he shoved his bare feet into the pair of athletic shoes he'd worn to the park. Only when he stepped outside and cool air blasted him did he remember he wore nothing other than cotton pajama bottoms beneath his jacket.

Sierra glanced up the moment his feet struck the wood-slat walkway, the clacking sound echoing in the still night. If she was surprised by his appearance, she gave no indication. Not even when he hopped over the low gate.

Jamie stopped crying upon spotting Clay but still fussed.

"You okay?"

It seemed as though he was always asking her that question. During their dinners together. After their counseling sessions. At the end of her work day. Before meeting his dad today.

"Jamie's been crying for the last two hours. I don't know what's wrong with him. The teething gel hasn't helped, if it's even that. He doesn't have a diaper rash. No fever. No stuffy nose. No throwing up." She jiggled him on her knees. "I wish you could talk, baby. Tell me what's wrong."

Jamie hiccupped and shuddered slightly as a muffled sob escaped.

"He probably had a rough day like the rest of us."

"And he's overtired. He didn't get much of

a nap this afternoon." She lifted by his under-arms and stood him on her thighs. "I came outside hoping the fresh air would relax him."

Clay considered offering to hold Jamie. Then, he had a better idea. "Why don't we take him inside the house?"

"Yours?"

"He can play with Oreo, and I'll make us cups of that herbal tea you like."

"I used my last teabag this morning."

"I have a box. Bought it at the store the other day."

"Really?"

He could tell the extra effort he'd taken on her behalf pleased her. "We could warm up a can of formula for Jamie."

"You have toddler formula, too?"

"I think that's what it is. There's a picture of a kid about Jamie's age on the label. Supposed to be more nutritious than plain milk."

"I suppose you have a bottle, too."

"As a matter of fact…" He'd been preparing for when Sierra was ready to leave Jamie with him for extended periods.

Or when she moved out into her own place and Jamie stayed with Clay on "his days." Just because things were progressing extraordinarily well was no guarantee they'd stay that way.

He and Sierra hadn't kissed since that night by Jamie's crib. Not that Clay didn't want to or didn't think about kissing her. Day in, day out. But Jamie was their priority and main focus.

"Come on, let's go." He inclined his head toward the house.

She wavered.

He stood, held out a hand to her. She allowed him to assist her to her feet.

Her fingers were small and soft and warm inside his.

Jamie's fussiness ceased the instant they entered the house. The fluorescent lights in the kitchen seemed to fascinate him. Tilting his head back, he gawked at the ceiling.

Sierra gawked at Clay, making him a tad self-conscious. He'd taken off his jacket and left his shoes by the door, forgetting that all he wore were his cotton pajama bottoms.

Well, she'd seen him in less before. A lot less.

He boiled water for the tea while Sierra set Jamie on the floor and prepared his bottle of toddler formula. He lost interest in the lights the moment Oreo meandered into the kitchen. The dog licked Jamie's face, then bowed down in a huge stretch and yawned expansively.

Clay patted Oreo's head. "I see one of us isn't having trouble sleeping."

When the tea was ready, he transferred the steaming mugs to the table. Sierra tried to pick up Jamie, but he scrambled away from her. Rather than fight, she gave him the bottle, which he drank while sitting on the floor next to Oreo.

"I've been thinking about what your dad said today." She plucked nervously at her oversize T-shirt and sweatpants.

Clay was going to bring up the wild-mustang auction. This was an unexpected, and better, subject. "You want to discuss it?"

She grimaced. "You sound like Dr. Brewster."

"Sorry." The counseling sessions had definitely influenced him. "Thanks again for letting my dad meet Jamie. Not that you care, but it meant a lot to him."

"I did it for Jamie."

"And me?"

She averted her gaze.

Sometimes saying nothing spoke volumes.

"I don't expect you to forgive him," Clay said.

"Have you?"

Clay spoke slowly, aware that if he leveled

with Sierra he'd be treading on dangerous ground. "I'm trying. We've had some conversations lately. There's more to my parents' split than either of them told me."

"Isn't that common in divorce?"

True. He'd certainly kept facts about his own divorce private. Never at the expense of another person, however.

"My mom let me make assumptions about my dad and didn't correct them. Harmful assumptions."

"Why would she do that?"

"Their divorce was complicated. She was angry at him. When I confronted her with what my dad said, she admitted misleading me."

Sierra shook her head. "I can't see your mom lying."

"She didn't lie so much as omit."

"They divorced years ago. Why is this even important?"

"Closure, I suppose. It started when I told Dad about Jamie. Apparently my parents didn't want to drag me into the nasty details of their divorce or acknowledge the mistakes they'd made."

"Like your dad selling my family's land to an investor?"

Up till now, Clay had danced around the subject of Wayne. He decided the time had come for frankness. "There's more to the sale of your family's land than either of our parents told us. Ask your dad."

"What purpose would that serve?"

"Learning the truth."

She snorted indignantly. "The truth is your father breached the contract he had with mine. Just because he didn't think he had a choice doesn't make it acceptable or forgivable."

"Sierra—"

"My dad was depressed for years. He's finally his old self again. I'm not risking a relapse by hammering him with questions about the darkest days of his life."

"Okay. I didn't mean to push you." Clay had been struggling to temper that least-desirable trait of his.

"And I didn't mean to get defensive."

They sipped their tea wordlessly for several seconds.

Sierra broke the lull. "What do you want from our relationship, Clay?"

"To be great parents to Jamie."

"Is that all?"

Dr. Brewster had encouraged direct questions. Sierra was apparently taking the advice seriously.

"If we weren't already in an unconventional relationship, I'd pursue a conventional one."

"You'd ask me out?"

"Yes."

"But we *do* have an unconventional relationship."

He turned the tables on her. "What are you really asking?"

She sighed, propped her chin on her hand. "Things keep changing on me. The last two years have been a roller-coaster ride. I know I want stability and permanence, for me and for Jamie."

"You don't have that here?"

"Come on. There are two legal agreements binding us together and both of them expire at the end of three months. That's not exactly permanence."

"I won't kick you out of the casita or fire you."

"You say that now. What if you meet someone?"

"That isn't likely."

"You've said that before."

She had every reason to doubt him. He'd

given Sierra a similar assurance right before reconciling with Jessica. "Can we take this one day at a time? Not worry about what hasn't happened and probably won't?"

"You're right." She sighed.

Could she be searching for more than permanence? A home rather than a place to live? A career with potential rather than a plain old job? A loving, committed relationship rather than a man with whom she shared parenting duties?

Clay's aversion to marriage had lessened considerably in recent weeks, but he still remained cautious. Sierra was astute and probably sensed his reservations.

"I'm attracted to you," he said, gauging her reaction. "I think that's obvious."

"A little." She smiled. A spark lit her eyes.

His pulse jumped. "Unconventional relationship or not, we could still go out."

"As in a date?"

Start with a date, he was thinking, but said, "Yeah. Take Jamie along."

Her smile turned mischievous. "Then it wouldn't be much of a date. What if I want to go to a grown-up restaurant, not a pizza place with games and ten million screaming kids?"

His pulse went from jumping to leaping. "You okay with someone watching him?"

"Your mom or my dad. For a couple of hours."

What would Dr. Brewster's reaction be to them going on a date? What about their attorneys?

"Ah!" Sierra's expression melted. "Would you look at that."

Clay followed her gaze to Jamie, sound asleep on the floor beside Oreo. The dog, snoring quietly, rested his head on Jamie's bottom.

"I should put him to bed."

"Wait. Not yet." Clay retrieved his smart phone from the counter and snapped several pictures.

"You're not going to email those to all your friends and family and post them on Facebook?"

"What kind of dad would I be if I didn't?"

"I want copies, too."

When he finished with the pictures, she bent and tugged Jamie out from under Oreo.

The dog grunted his displeasure at the loss of his pillow.

"Where'd I leave that blanket?" She glanced around, Jamie draped limply over her shoulder.

"Don't leave yet."

"It's almost midnight."

"You haven't finished your tea." Or their conversation. "The cold air might wake him up."

"Umm…"

"Put him in the playpen."

"You have a playpen? Where?"

"In the living room. I just bought it."

"Along with the toddler formula and bottles?"

"And some more baby junk."

"Just how much baby junk did you buy?"

Clay grinned like a boy on his first pony ride. "Put Jamie in the playpen and I'll show you."

Chapter Twelve

Sierra waited while Clay spread an old afghan in the bottom of the playpen. She laid Jamie on top of it and used a corner to cover him up.

Amazingly, he didn't stir once.

"Where are all these new purchases?" she whispered as they padded on bare feet to the hall.

"This way."

Clay took her to the den. There, on the couch, were bags and bags of baby things. On the floor beside the couch was a tricycle.

"You've really outdone yourself." Sierra went to the tricycle and lifted one of the brightly colored streamers hanging from the handlebars. "He's not quite old enough for this. Or this." She dug out a skateboard and rolled her eyes. "And here I thought a pony was bad."

"I bought a helmet and knee pads. They're in one of the bags."

"Clay Duvall, you're impossible." She laughed. Easily, naturally. Wasn't that a nice change from the glum mood she'd been in after the picnic at the park?

"Granted, I may have gotten carried away," he confessed.

"You think?" Still laughing, she came over and pressed a hand to his cheek. "You're a very a sweet man. Jamie's a fortunate boy to have you for his father. Not just because of what you can buy him—" She moved her hand from his cheek to his chest and laid it over his heart. "Because you love him."

"Thank you. For Jamie and for working so hard to make this relationship of ours work."

"It's not as bad as I thought it would be."

"No, it isn't."

Her gaze roved his face, settled on his eyes. This was no trust exercise. She looked at him for the sheer pleasure it gave her.

Drawn by an irresistible pull, she swayed toward him.

He circled her waist with his arms, narrowing the distance between them to nothing. "Sierra, I—"

"Don't say anything." She pressed a finger to his mouth. "Show me instead."

He groaned and brushed his lips across hers, slowly, purposefully. She leaned into him, fitted her body to his and pressed her breasts against him. The passion that had swept them up before instantly reignited.

Two years ago, Clay had desired her. Not because he loved her or even wanted her. He'd been needing a balm to soothe the ache left by Jessica. Sierra had been available and willing to provide that balm.

Tonight was different.

Jessica was buried deep in Clay's past where she belonged. It was Sierra's name Clay murmured as he trailed kisses along her jaw and down her throat. It was her eyes he lost himself in before claiming her mouth again. It was her desperate need he was eager to satisfy.

Emotions gathered inside her, then tumbled out in a shiver that left her simultaneously weak-kneed and exhilarated.

Clay ruthlessly broke off their kiss, gasping for air as if every molecule of oxygen had been sucked from the room.

He tried to talk and couldn't.

She enjoyed leaving him speechless.

"We'd better stop while I can," he managed in a choked voice.

"Do you want to stop?"

"What do you think?"

She thought he'd like to take her to bed.

Were they ready?

This was new territory they were navigating, despite having slept together before. Common sense dictated they proceed slowly.

Sierra had been listening to her common sense for two years and was tired of it.

"I could go, but I hate to wake up Jamie."

"If you stay, I don't want Jamie to be the reason."

If she stayed, there would be no going back. Ever.

His breathing steadied, and his muscles relaxed.

She liked him better when that infuriating control of his was about to snap.

"It would be a shame to wake him up." She smiled seductively.

"A crying shame." Clay hauled her off her feet for another kiss and carried her down the hall.

His bedroom was large and the decor masculine, like the rest of his house.

The bed was simply too far away and Sierra in too much of a hurry.

"Put me down."

Clay set her on her feet in the middle of the room. She didn't wait for him to undress her but tugged off her T-shirt.

"Wow." He filled his hands with her breasts. "You are gorgeous."

She felt gorgeous. And daring and, yes, timid. She was taking a chance, putting her heart out there again with no protection.

"I won't hurt you, I promise."

Her fears must have shown on her face.

She covered his hands with hers, let the silky sensations his touch evoked slide through her.

"Let's just concentrate on the here and now," she said. "Not worry about what hasn't happened."

Hadn't he told her the very same thing earlier?

He kissed her mouth, her shoulders, tickled the tops of her breasts with his five o'clock shadow. His restraint was maddening. When had he gained control and she lost hers?

"Clay, please." She arched her back, and he reached between her legs.

"What do you want? Tell me."

"You, naked, inside me."

They tumbled onto the bed, the rest of their clothes dissolving in a mad frenzy. When she would have straddled him, Clay took his time exploring every inch of her with intimate touches and sensual caresses. Not to mention kisses. Lots of them. All over.

Her hands weren't still, either. She traced the contour of his broad chest, his lean thighs, his tight buttocks. His body had always fascinated her, and she reveled in the rediscovery.

She bit his earlobe as her fingers found his erection. "I want you inside me."

"Not half as much as I want you."

Rolling onto his side, he opened the drawer of the nightstand and removed a condom. Swiftly covering his erection, he pushed her onto her back and entered her.

Sierra gasped in astonishment and delight, rising off the mattress as every one of her muscles contracted. The next instant, her limbs turned to liquid as he thrust in and out of her, his rhythm steadily increasing at the same rate as her excitement.

Heaven help her, she wanted more.

"Touch me."

At her bold demand, he drove into her harder, his hand stroking her where she craved it the most.

The connection was electrifying.

Within seconds, she reached a spectacular climax that triggered an onslaught of emotions. Tears sprang to her eyes. She blinked them away, hoping Clay wouldn't notice.

He did. "What's this?" He wiped her moist cheek.

She started to tell him it was nothing. Except that would be a terrible lie.

"Make love to me." That was as near as she could come to telling him what lay in her heart.

His breathing grew shallower, and his thrusts went deeper. She clung to him, told him how incredible he felt and how good they were together.

He shuddered, buried his face in her neck and let go.

She enjoyed his release almost as much as she had her own. Clay might be bigger and stronger than her, but she was capable of reducing him to a weakling simply by moving her hips a certain way.

"Stop that," he growled, "unless you mean

business." He captured her wrist and brought her hand to his mouth.

She sifted her fingers through his short disheveled hair. "I'm glad Jamie was fussy tonight."

"You have no idea how often I've wanted to walk over to that casita." His smile was little-boy charming.

"I'm not sure the evening would have ended the same if you did."

"Me either, to be honest." He rolled off her onto his side.

Sierra missed him immediately and was glad when he scooped her into his arms. She reciprocated by curling her leg around his calf.

"This is nice," he said, his voice tinged with sleep.

Sierra was suddenly tired, too, and her own eyelids drifted shut.

The day had been filled with ups and down, highs and lows and unexpected turns. Being physically sated contributed to her sleepiness. So did being cocooned in Clay's arms.

She'd started to drift off when he kissed the back of her neck. "I have an idea."

"Mmm, what's that?"

"Let's get married."

Her eyes flew open, and she came instantly wide awake.

Sierra sat up and swung her legs over the side of the mattress, her back to Clay. "That was out of the blue."

"Was it?" He propped himself up on one elbow and stroked her arm, the sleepiness vanished from his voice. "Can you honestly tell me you haven't thought about marrying me?"

She had, a lot. Two years ago. She'd dreamed of nothing else after returning to San Francisco. Even when she heard he and Jessica had reconciled, a small part of her hoped they'd break up again. Then, she'd received two stunning blows. She was pregnant, and, a week later, she learned Clay and Jessica were engaged.

"It's too soon for us to think about marriage. This… We…" Sierra waved a hand at the bed. "Everything is happening really fast. We haven't gone on our first date yet."

"Jamie is our son. You and he are my family. I think it would be best for him if we were married. You said you wanted stability and permanence."

All right, people married for the sake of their child every day. Clay's proposal wasn't as out of the blue as she'd claimed. But Jamie wasn't enough of a reason for her to accept. Clay felt compelled to "do the right thing," which was why she hadn't told him about her pregnancy in the beginning.

"I do want stability and permanence," she said. "I also want to marry for love. To be in a committed relationship with a man who adores me and can't bear to live without me."

"I adore you, Sierra. You're a beautiful, smart, talented woman. An incredible mother. Everything I want in a wife."

Do you love me?

He hadn't included that in his list of the perfect-wife qualities.

Do I love him?

She did. Despite all the doubts and uncertainties, she'd been steadily falling for Clay since her return home. If she didn't love him, she wouldn't be in his bed now.

"Hey, come on, look at me." He reached up and, taking her chin between his fingers, forced her to look at him.

His vulnerable expression turned her insides to mush.

"Won't you at least consider my proposal?" he asked.

"I'm not ready. We have too many unresolved issues."

There was sufficient moonlight streaming in though the shutters for her to discern the flare of disappointment in his eyes. Had she crushed his ego or did he truly care for her?

He must. No man made love with the kind of intense passion Clay did without caring for his partner.

She'd feel a whole lot better about them and their future if he'd say those three little words.

"I'm touched by your proposal." She cupped his cheek, attempting to restore their former mood.

"I can see where I might have jumped the gun."

"You do that sometimes." Though there was a big difference between buying a one-year-old a tricycle and proposing marriage.

"The control freak strikes again."

She smiled. "You said it, not me."

He returned her smile. "Why don't we just live together?"

"Live together," she repeated slowly.

"Yeah. We practically already are."

"No, we're not." She stiffened. "We have completely separate residences."

He sat up beside her, his thigh brushing hers. "What's wrong?"

"You're pressuring me."

"Take your time deciding. I'm in no rush."

"I'm not sure of your motives."

"For asking you to move in with me?"

"That and proposing."

"I told you, Jamie and you."

Right. To give her stability and permanence. Not for love.

Another legal agreement binding them together. This one a marriage license.

She should drop the subject before either of them said something they'd regret.

He tucked a lock of hair behind her ear. "If I'm pressuring you it's because you mean the world to me, and I don't want to lose you."

Funny, she was afraid of losing him.

"That still isn't a good reason to get married or move in together. Those are huge steps."

"You're right. It's just that tonight was amazing. Not only the sex. And make no mistake, that was mind-blowing. I'm talking about the emotional connection. I've never felt so close to anyone."

Almost a declaration of love.

Maybe he was one of those men who couldn't say it out loud.

"Oh, Clay." She bent and kissed his cheek. "I'm sorry I botched this."

"You didn't. You've let me know we have enough between us to build a solid relationship. We love Jamie and want what's best for him. We also have some pretty powerful feelings for each other. Maybe, if we go slow, we can have something really special one day."

"I said you were smart." He kissed her mouth thoroughly. "Will you at least spend the night with me?"

She laughed and slid her foot along his thigh. "I'm not going anywhere, cowboy."

And she didn't, for another hour.

After a second round of love-making, Sierra tiptoed to the living room and checked on Jamie. He continued sleeping peacefully in the playpen, Oreo on the floor beside him.

She scratched the dog's ear. "Watch out for him, will you?"

Oreo's tail thumped.

Rather than immediately return to bed, Sierra stood over Jamie, considering the night's events yet again.

She had thought herself the insecure one,

plagued by doubts and anxieties, and Clay the confident, self-assured one. Yet, he wasn't always confident and self-assured.

Which might explain why he had reconciled with Jessica rather than attempt a long-distance relationship with Sierra. And why he always strived to be in control. He was compensating for his fears.

The two of them were a study in contradictions.

She sighed. This new relationship of theirs would either be a stupendous success or an equally stupendous failure.

"I'm pretty sure the three of us bought out the entire store!" Sage laughed as she climbed awkwardly into the front passenger seat of Sierra's SUV, her growing stomach hampering her movements.

"If you don't tell Ethan, I won't tell Gavin." Caitlin made funny faces at Jamie as she hopped in the back seat next to him.

Sierra buckled the harness on his car seat and shut the door.

She and her sisters-in-law had spent the entire morning shopping at baby boutiques in nearby Scottsdale. Actually, Sage and Caitlin had done most of the shopping. After only a month at the rodeo arena, part-time at that, Sierra was still carefully managing her disposable income.

Clay would buy her anything she had a hankering for, and that was the problem. She didn't want to take advantage of him. Their *dating* relationship, while in the early stages, was going well. More than well, in fact, and she'd hate to mess it up by giving him reasons to think her feelings for him were based solely on what he could provide her.

"I'm not ready to go home yet," Sage announced. "Are you?" She looked to Sierra and Caitlin for confirmation.

"Me, either." Caitlin yawned and stretched. She'd only recently started showing, and most of her purchases today were maternity clothes.

"You sure? You look tired."

"Nothing a little pick-me-up won't cure. Anyone hungry?"

"Starving!" Sage rubbed her belly. "Junior, too. Why don't we stop for lunch at the Corner Diner?"

"What do you say, Sierra?" Caitlin smiled winningly. "My treat, in exchange for you driving us around all morning."

Sierra glanced over her shoulder at Jamie.

He was as energized as his Aunt Sage and as content as his Aunt Caitlin. "Sure. Why not?"

Twenty-five minutes later they were being seated at the busy diner, Jamie in one of the restaurant-provided high chairs. Sierra automatically dug several of his toys out from the diaper bag. He was far more interested in the plastic-laminated dessert menu.

Once they placed their orders with the waitress, the conversation returned to where it had been most of the morning—babies.

"Did you know you were having a boy?" Caitlin asked. "Ethan wants to find out the baby's sex, but I don't."

"I refuse to find out," Sage chimed in. "We already have two girls. I'm worried Gavin will be disappointed if we have another one."

"Oh, Gavin won't care." Caitlin dismissed her sister-in-law with a shrug, and, thank goodness, forgot about Sierra.

She'd dreaded having to answer the question. It brought back too many sad memories. Once she'd agreed to the adoption, the Stevensons had insisted on learning if her baby was a boy or a girl, even accompanying Sierra to an ultrasound appointment.

Knowing she was carrying a boy had made those last few months of Sierra's pregnancy excruciatingly difficult. She was no longer carrying a baby, she was carrying her son.

A son she was abandoning.

"How're things going with you and Clay?" Sage asked, nibbling a cracker. She gave one to Jamie.

This question was easier to answer, yet Sierra hedged. What if talking about her and Clay jinxed their relationship?

"Fine."

"That's all?"

"Okay, really fine."

Clay had broken the news that he and Sierra were seeing each other to Sierra's brothers. Ethan had been happy for them. Gavin, as usual, expressed reservations.

"Have you moved in with him yet? What?" Caitlin objected when Sage sent her a warning glance. "Am I being too nosy?"

"I'm still in the casita and he's still in his house."

Technically, that was true. Sierra insisted on maintaining her residence in the casita in order to minimize disrupting Jamie's schedule. Clay hadn't insisted on taking Jamie during "his days," though he could if he chose to enforce the custody agreement.

"We eat breakfast together every morning and dinner together every evening. In his house," she added. "We also have Friday date nights and family Sundays."

And, almost always, Clay spent the night in the casita with her. That probably wouldn't last much longer. Jamie was getting too big to be sleeping in the same room with his parents.

The thought of him occupying his own room didn't distress Sierra anymore, thanks to her counseling.

Or maybe the reason was sharing her bed with Clay. She definitely felt calmer and slept better snuggled against him.

What she refused to tell her sisters-in-law was that the last family Sunday had been spent with Bud Duvall, this time at an indoor playground with an activity center designed for toddlers.

If Sage and Caitlin found out, they'd spill the beans to Sierra's brothers, and she wasn't ready to deal with the inevitable fallout. Ethan might understand but Gavin and her father would come unglued.

She couldn't keep it from them forever. Jamie was quickly coming to adore his other grandfather. Bud had won him over at the playground by climbing into the ball pit with him and chasing him through the tunnels.

For her part, Sierra continued having trouble reconciling the horrible man who'd destroyed her family with the kind, caring grandfather who doted on his grandson.

"How's the job going?" Caitlin asked.

"I love it." Sierra smiled broadly, glad for the distraction. "The work's really interesting, and there's a lot of it. I'm busy every minute."

"I'm jealous," Sage said. "You get to take Jamie with you to the office. I'll have to leave Junior here in day care or—" she sighed despairingly "—with Gavin."

"It's not always easy, believe me. Jamie can be very demanding. And loud. It's embarrassing when I'm on the phone and he starts wailing."

She should arrange day care. But every time she imagined leaving Jamie with someone else, she was reminded of the Stevensons and panicked.

"I'm thinking of hiring Cassie this summer to watch him while I work."

Sierra and Gavin's daughter had engaged in a long talk after the wedding. They'd both regretted the incident and wanted to make amends.

"That's a wonderful solution," Sage gushed.

Yeah, other than Cassie wouldn't be off school for three more months. Thank goodness Clay was patient.

"How's the wild-horse auction coming?" Sage asked. "I can't believe it's in two weeks. I'm so excited. I wish I could be more involved."

"We're on target. The horses are ready. We've hired the auctioneer. Arranged for Cassie's equestrian drill team to run the concession stand. My big concern is publicity. Ads are appearing in the newspapers this week and next, and I've contacted five local TV stations. So far, only one has committed. I worry I haven't done enough."

"Gavin tells me Prince is ready for his picture-taking," Sage said. "They've been practicing."

Sierra was less sure. About Prince, not Dallas. She and the photographer had gotten to know each other over the last couple weeks and had become friends. Sierra was mortified to think she once suspected Dallas of going after Clay.

Their food arrived, and Sage dove into her sandwich with gusto. "This is delicious."

"Hey, I've just had the best idea." Caitlin

put down her fork and grabbed Sage's arm. "Let's throw Jamie a belated birthday party."

"Yes, we should!"

"No, no," Sierra protested. "He doesn't need any more presents. Clay's bought him too many already."

"But not the rest of his family," Caitlin insisted. "We want to dote on him, too."

Sierra wavered, remembering Gail Stevenson's baby shower. She'd tried to coerce Sierra into attending, but she simply couldn't bring herself to go. That evening, Gail had shown Sierra all the baby gifts her family and friends had given her, never noticing Sierra's anguish.

"You have enough on your plates already," Sierra insisted, "getting ready for your own babies."

"Are you kidding?" Sage exclaimed. "It'll be a blast. We'll have it next weekend. Before the horse auction."

"Is that enough time?"

"Plenty."

"I don't know."

"Please, Sierra." Caitlin touched her arm. "The party isn't just for Jamie. It's for all of us. We love him and you."

How could Sierra say no to that? "All right."

Sage and Caitlin chatted enthusiastically about the party, with Sierra insisting they limit the guest list to a reasonable number.

"My mom will want to come." Caitlin had taken out a pen and paper and was making notes.

Jamie, who'd been good as gold till now, decided to drop his spoon and bowl of applesauce on the floor.

Sierra leaned over to retrieve it. She sat up and saw a hostess escorting two women to a booth. Her breath caught as she recognized the younger one.

Jessica Rovedatti. Or Jessica Duvall if she hadn't taken back her maiden name after her divorce from Clay.

An invisible wall of ice slammed into her, shaking her to her core.

Sierra set the bowl and spoon on the table, fumbling slightly.

"Honey, are you okay?" Caitlin asked.

"I'm… Um, yeah."

Caitlin turned her head and hissed, "Oh, my God! I don't believe it."

She'd recognized Clay's ex-wife, having grown up in the area and dated Ethan for years.

"What?" Sage shifted in her seat to see. "Who?"

"Please," Sierra implored in a hushed voice. "I don't want her looking over here."

Too late. Jessica acknowledged Sierra with a cool nod, no smile, and returned her attention to her lunch companion.

Sierra drew in a shaky breath.

"Who is she?" Sage demanded.

Caitlin pushed aside her empty plate. "Clay's ex-wife."

"Oh. *Ooohh*. I thought she lived in Texas."

So had Sierra.

"Wonder what she's doing here?" Caitlin peered across the dining room, trying to be discreet and not succeeding.

Sierra clasped Jamie's hand protectively in hers, the image of Jessica's cool nod replaying over and over inside her head.

The waitress couldn't come fast enough with their tab.

Chapter Thirteen

Sierra put Jamie down for his nap shortly after returning from the diner. Taking the nursery monitor with her, she crossed the backyard and went into the house.

"You home?" she hollered.

"Hey!" Clay's voice carried from the living room. "In here."

She found him on the floor, surrounded by an assortment of large plastic pieces and a sheet of instructions lying open beside him. He wore basketball shorts, a sweatshirt with the sleeves cut off and a backward baseball cap. A far cry from his typical cowboy shirt and jeans.

If she weren't upset over seeing Jessica at the diner, she'd joke with him about his attire.

"What are you doing?"

"Putting this together." He pointed to an empty cardboard box. On the side was a picture of a miniature slide and a child going down it, his arms lifted high over his head. "He had such a good time at the indoor playground, I thought he'd like this."

She wanted to admonish Clay for spoiling Jamie but held her tongue. "Where are you going to put it?"

"I thought on the back porch." He glanced at the nursery monitor in her hand. "Jamie asleep?"

"Yeah. He's wiped out after our shopping spree." She sat on the sofa and watched Clay. He assembled the slide with the meticulous attention of a master craftsman.

"Have fun with the girls?"

"I did." For most of the morning. "We had lunch at the Corner Diner."

He must have discerned the tiny note of distress in her voice for he asked, "Everything all right?"

"Something did happen."

"What?"

"Jessica was there. At the diner."

He set the plastic pieces he'd been holding aside. "She was?"

"Having lunch with a woman I didn't recognize. I'm surprised she's back in Mustang Valley. I thought her family moved to Avondale."

Clay picked up the slide pieces he'd set down and attempted to fit them together. When he spoke, his tone was measured. "She's in town visiting her godmother."

"You knew?"

"I talked to her recently."

The revelation shocked Sierra almost as much as seeing Jessica. "When?"

"She called last week to tell me she was coming to Arizona for a couple weeks."

"I see." Every insecurity Sierra had thought she'd beaten, every fear she'd set to rest, returned in one violent, blinding wave.

Clay had been in contact with Jessica. Behind Sierra's back!

"It's not unusual for divorced people to stay in touch," he said.

"Are you in touch with her a lot?"

"Once in a while we email or talk on the phone."

"You couldn't tell me this?"

"I didn't want to upset you."

"Is there anything else you're hiding from me?"

He got to his feet and joined her on the couch. "I'm not hiding anything from you. I swear."

Why then did she feel betrayed?

"Does she know about Jamie?"

"Yes."

"You told her when she called you last week."

"Before then."

Once in a while was beginning to sound like every week.

"I told her about *us* when I saw her the other day."

"You *saw* her?" Anger seeped in, filling the cracks he was leaving in her heart.

She couldn't sit here another second and listen to him try to convince her that communicating with Jessica was perfectly normal.

"There was a form she needed to sign so I could remove her as beneficiary on my life insurance policy and add you and Jamie."

He'd added *her* and Jamie as his beneficiaries? That took some of the wind from her sails.

"I could have shipped the form to her," Clay

went on to explain, "but when she said she was coming to town for a visit, I decided to handle it in person. Jessica's forgetful some-times, and I wanted to make the change now."

Everything Clay said made sense. And yet...

"Didn't you take her off your insurance policy when you divorced?"

"Honestly, it didn't occur to me until I went to renew the policy."

"Do you still love her?"

He reached up and rubbed his knuckles along Sierra's cheek. "I haven't loved her for a long, long time. But I did once, and she was a big part of my life for many years. It isn't always easy to let go, even in the wake of hurt and resentment."

"You can't let go of Jessica?" How could he still cling to her after what she'd done to him?

How could he ever love Sierra?

"Believe me, I have. She's just a person from my past. You and Jamie are my future."

Suddenly, comprehension dawned. "She's the one unable to let go of you."

"I think being single again isn't as much fun as she anticipated."

"Poor Jessica."

Clay pressed a light kiss to Sierra's mouth.

"You have nothing to worry about where she's concerned."

No? Jessica had always exuded a sort of power over Clay. He'd been crazy mad in love with her, and she'd expertly wrapped him around her little finger.

Sierra wanted her back in Texas in the worst way.

God, why had she agreed to joint custody? She should have fought tooth and nail for sole custody.

Then, she wouldn't be scared to death "the other woman" would be helping Clay raise Jamie on the days he had his son.

"Morning." Clay breezed into the kitchen, tucking his shirt into his jeans.

Sierra stood at the counter, fixing breakfast—for Jamie.

Not that Clay expected her to cook for him, they usually shared the chore. But since they'd taken their relationship to the next level, so to speak, whenever she scrambled eggs and toasted bread for Jamie, she made extra for Clay.

He could always have oatmeal in the office, he supposed.

"What's on your schedule for today?" he

asked, kissing the top of Jamie's head. The boy sat in his high chair, Oreo beside him, waiting for any food that found its way to the floor.

Clay would have kissed Sierra, too, but she'd remained aloof since yesterday afternoon and the Jessica conversation. What were the odds his girlfriend and his ex-wife would be at the diner the same time?

In hindsight, he should have told Sierra about Jessica's visit and the beneficiary form. Live and learn.

"I need to run to the discount store today for diapers and baby food," she said. "Then hit the office."

Pouring himself a cup of coffee, Clay sat at the table and combed his fingers through his shower-dampened hair. "I assume you're still mad at me."

"I'm not mad." She set a plate in front of Jamie. He immediately fed a toast triangle to Oreo. "No, honey bun, those are for you. Oreo's already had breakfast." She handed Jamie a baby spoon for his eggs.

He preferred using his fingers.

"You sure you're not mad?" Clay presented his most appealing smile. "Because you're acting it. I know you didn't sleep well last night."

"You explained everything. I have nothing to worry about, right?"

"Right."

She started loading the dishwasher. "Okay then."

It wasn't as if anything had happened with Jessica. She and Clay had met at a coffee shop, she'd signed the form, he'd showed her pictures of Jamie, they'd talked for ten minutes, and then he'd left.

Wait a minute! On second thought, something did happen. A big something. When he'd left the coffee shop, he didn't glance back once or give her a moment's consideration until Sierra mentioned seeing her.

What a relief. He hadn't lied. He was finally and truly over Jessica.

Before he could tell Sierra, her cell phone rang. She retrieved it from the counter and glanced at the caller ID, her expression puzzled.

"Hello. Yes, good morning," she said brightly after a pause. "I'm still interested." Casting Clay a guilty look, she walked into the family room, the phone pressed to her ear.

She didn't want Clay to hear her conversation. Naturally, his curiosity skyrocketed. He went over and played with Jamie, stealing bites of his eggs and toast, much to Jamie's amusement. Clay heard only a word here and there of Sierra's phone call, not enough to decipher it.

"Thank you very much for considering me," she said. "I look forward to the call."

Clay clearly heard that last part and frowned.

She returned to the kitchen, murmuring, "Sorry about that," and resumed loading the dishwasher.

The hell with respecting her privacy. "Was that about a job?"

She pivoted to face him, her mouth set in a determined line. "Yes."

Holy cow, she was really mad at him.

"I didn't realize you were looking for a new one."

"I'm not. This is a company I applied to before I started working for you. They're hiring a new position and going through the résumés on file."

"Are you seriously considering it?" The few bites of Jamie's breakfast Clay had eaten sat like stones in his stomach. She was quitting him.

"It pays well and the hours are flexible."

"I'll give you a raise."

She exhaled sharply. "It's just a phone interview. I'm one of a dozen."

"We have an agreement." He was ashamed at himself for sinking so low as to use their employment contract.

"This job doesn't start till May, after the contract expires."

"It automatically renews."

"If I don't opt out."

"Are you ready to put Jamie in day care?"

"I think I will be by then."

"You're doing this because of Jessica."

"She has *nothing* to do with me considering a potential job opportunity."

"Yes, she does. You're mad because I met her the other day and didn't tell you."

"I don't care who you—" She stopped, let her shoulders sag. "That's not true. I do care. Jessica is a sore spot with me. But I'm not mad at you, just hurt."

Clay rose from his chair and crossed the kitchen in three strides. Wrapping his arms around Sierra's waist, he pulled her to him.

"You have every right to be hurt. I was an insensitive dope. I thought I was avoiding an argument with you. Instead, I lost your trust."

"You haven't lost my trust. Maybe dented it."

"I promise, if I see or hear from Jessica again, not that I plan to, I'll tell you." He squeezed Sierra tight, needing her to squeeze him in return. She didn't. "Interview with the company. If they make you an offer, I only ask you give me a chance to beat it."

"We'll see."

He set her away from him and studied her face. "You won't?"

"No, I'll see about interviewing. I'm not that interested in the job."

He kissed her, drank her in, was reborn when she at last responded.

Given his choice, he'd carry her to his bedroom, make endless love to her until he wiped Jessica completely from her mind and heart. Unfortunately, they couldn't leave Jamie in his high chair and there were a half dozen phone calls waiting for him to place the second he set foot in the office.

"I'll see you later." He nuzzled her ear before reluctantly releasing her.

She usually giggled when he did that and told him not to tickle her.

"I'll be in after lunch. I have to type up those new contracts for your signature. And I'm hoping to hear back from the TV stations.

Did I tell you I might have a lead on some grant money?"

She was all business. Normally, Clay liked talking shop with her. Today, it felt as if she'd erected a ten-foot wall to keep him at a distance and her heart safe.

Sierra perched on the wingback chair in her family's living room, a pile of unopened gifts on one side of her, a pile of opened gifts on the other. Jamie sat on the floor, shredding wrapping paper and unraveling bows. When Cassie and Isa weren't fussing over him, they picked through the gifts, deciding which one Sierra should open next.

The women guests huddled close to her, oohing and ahhing at the appropriate moments. The men occupied the farther corners of the room, conversing amongst themselves and participating as little as possible.

Sierra was reminded of the wedding last month when Caitlin and Sage had sat in this same room, opening their gifts. She couldn't believe all the trouble they'd gone through for her. In a week, they'd pulled together a baby shower that was better than anything she could have hoped for.

The Powell house and ranch, a sad and

lonely place for so many years, was bursting with people and activity and, most importantly, love. Not to mention children. From none to five in barely over a year. That had to be some kind of record.

Seeing her brothers and father content warmed Sierra's heart. She'd been happy like them for a while, too. Then, she'd found out Jessica was back in Mustang Valley and Clay had had a meeting with her. Sierra really didn't think anything had transpired between them other than signing the form.

It was the what-might-happen that had her sleeping poorly, phone-interviewing for a job she had no interest in and watching Clay's every move, searching for telltale signs that he was sneaking away to be with Jessica.

"Open this one." Cassie set a large box in front of Sierra. "It's from Grandpa."

She pasted a happy smile on her face and attacked the wrapping paper. "Dad, this is huge and heavy." The plain cardboard box containing the gift revealed nothing about its contents.

"I hope Jamie likes it," he said.

Sierra cut through the tape, opened the top of the box and peered inside. "What! You didn't." She rolled her eyes. He was absolutely hopeless. "A saddle? You bought him a saddle?"

Jamie came over to investigate.

"Let me see that." Clay scooted forward from where he'd been sitting on the couch. He pulled a child-size saddle from the box, holding on to it by the horn for everyone to see. "Look, Jamie, now all we need is a pony."

"No pony!" Sierra protested.

The women agreed. The men acted like they didn't hear.

"Thanks, Wayne," Clay said, still admiring the saddle and showing it to Jamie.

"Yeah, thanks, Dad," Sierra muttered.

"I didn't know what toys to get him." Her father's pleased-with-himself grin stretched from ear to ear.

"I'm surprised no one here got Jamie boots," Blythe remarked.

Ethan's face instantly drooped.

Sierra glowered at him. "Don't tell me."

"A cowboy needs boots."

Sierra wanted to be mad, but it was impossible in the presence of such love and generosity. She was truly blessed.

"Open this one." Isa handed Sierra a shirt box wrapped in paper with cartoon horses galloping over plains. "It doesn't say who it's from."

A card lay atop a miniature cowboy outfit, complete with Western shirt, jeans and even chaps, all about three sizes too big for Jamie.

"How adorable," Caitlin crooned.

Isa held the card out to Sierra.

"You go ahead and read it, honey." She was busy admiring the chaps, which appeared custom-made.

"It says 'to Jamie from Grandpa.'"

"Dad! Another present?"

"Huh?" Wayne squinted at the card. "I didn't buy that."

A jolt went through Sierra, and the chaps fell into her lap.

Not now, not yet, not today.

Her gaze flew to Clay. He knew, too.

Before either of them could react, Blythe dropped the bombshell. "It's from Jamie's other grandfather. He asked me to bring it."

"Other grandfather?" Isa examined the card as if it held the answer.

No one else spoke. Moved. Breathed.

"Yes, dear. Clay's father."

"Dammit to hell!" Gavin slapped his thighs and shot from his chair. "What's that bastard doing sending Jamie a present?"

"Sweetheart, the girls." Sage's eyes cut to their daughters.

Blythe looked stricken. Her fingers covered her mouth, and her cheeks drained of color.

Sierra's father's cheeks flushed a vivid red.

As if by silent consensus, everyone not a Powell or Duvall or married to one left the room.

"Cassie, would you and Isa take Jamie to the den for me, please?" Sierra was amazed at the steadiness of her voice.

They did as she asked, grabbing some of the new toys.

"Why would Duvall send a gift?" Gavin repeated. He was up and pacing the floor.

"He's Jamie's grandfather," Clay said.

"I wish he wasn't."

"Gavin!" Sage gasped.

"That man is a snake."

"Watch what you say," Clay warned, rising from the sofa. "You may be my business partner and buddy but I won't tolerate you insulting my family."

"I thought you hated him, too."

"I don't. I was angry at him. But I've since learned he's not entirely responsible for what happened to you."

"You're screwed in the head if you think that."

"Enough," Ethan barked at Gavin. "Sit down, both of you, and shut up."

"You're siding with Clay?"

"I'm refereeing."

Clay sat. Gavin resumed pacing.

"I'm sorry," Blythe murmured miserably. "When he asked me to deliver the gift, I didn't think it would be a problem. Considering you've reconciled, and he's been seeing Jamie."

"You let him near Jamie?" Gavin raged at Sierra. "How could you?"

She straightened her spine defensively. "I know how you feel about Bud—"

"I assumed I felt the same as you."

"It's my fault," Clay interjected. "I insisted on Jamie meeting my dad. Sierra didn't want him to."

"But you still allowed it?" Gavin demanded of her.

He was Sierra's big brother, used to ordering her around. She was tired of it, of all the men in her life thinking they knew what was best for her, including her old boss. Who was Ken Stevenson to judge how fit she'd be as a mother?

"I did allow it, and I'm glad. Bud is a good grandfather to Jamie."

"He's a thief."

Sierra stood and glared at Gavin, hands on her hips. She refused to let him intimidate her. "He gave us fifteen more months with Mom we wouldn't have had without that heart transplant."

"Then he stole our land."

"He did no such thing." All eyes turned to Sierra's father, his earlier flush replaced by a mask of pain and devastation. "I lost our land."

"What are you talking about?" Some of the razor-sharp steel had left Gavin's voice.

Yes, Sierra thought, what *was* her father talking about?

"Never mind." He turned his head to stare out the window.

"Wayne." Clay's gentle tone was in stark contrast to all the yelling. "It's time. They have a right to know, and you have a duty to tell them."

Her father coughed, and Sierra saw he was biting back a sob.

"It's all right, Dad."

"No. Nothing's been right for years."

His listlessness reminded her too much of

those desperate days during his depression. "You don't have to say anything."

"I couldn't make the payments. The loan was due, then overdue, then long overdue." He cleared his throat, sniffed, returned his attention to the room. "Bud gave me plenty of chances. I didn't take them. I'd lost your mother, lost myself to grief, then the business. I couldn't have scraped enough money together to buy back ten acres, much less all six hundred. I was sure if you kids found out, you'd leave me, too, like your mother did, and I'd be all alone."

"You *let* him sell our land?" Gavin's incredulousness mirrored Sierra's and everyone else's.

Her father was mistaken. Confused. He wouldn't have intentionally allowed an investor to buy their land and then tell everyone Bud stole it. That would be…a lie.

"Dad," she insisted, "don't feel the need to cover for Bud just because I let him see Jamie."

"I'm not covering for Bud." Her father's sad gaze pleaded for understanding. "He's covering for me."

"You're wrong, he stole our land. Who

would allow people to think the worst of them all these years if they did nothing wrong?"

"Someone who's a better friend to me than I was to him."

Sierra covered her face with her hands.

Gavin sat on the couch, then sank defeated into the cushions.

"I'm the one responsible," Blythe said softly, her eyes misting. "I didn't realize Bud would have to sell your land to settle our divorce. I thought you were making the payments."

"Not your fault, either, Blythe. I should have leveled with my kids. Been honest from the start."

Conversation continued around Sierra, but she hardly heard a word.

Her father, not Bud, was responsible for them losing their land. Their cattle business. Their reputation. Their heritage. How could he? And how could he have committed such an appalling injustice to a friend? A man who'd given him money for his wife's heart transplant surgery.

"I apologize, Clay. And to you, Blythe."

They assured Sierra's father they held no grudge against him.

What about Sierra and her brothers? Didn't their father owe them an apology, too?

Their lives would have been entirely different if he'd told the truth. Her brothers and Clay would have remained friends rather than become enemies. She and Clay wouldn't have had to hide their affair. He and Bud wouldn't have been estranged for years. She could have come home when she got pregnant instead of giving Jamie up for adoption.

Oh, God, what had her father done?

She thought of Clay's betrayal when he'd reconciled with Jessica and married her. It was nothing compared to this. He hadn't wiped out two families.

Suddenly chilled to the bone, Sierra rubbed her upper arms.

"Dad felt awful about having to sell your land," Clay said. "He wanted to extend the loan again, but he lost money in the stock market."

Sierra's hands stilled. "You knew about this?"

"Dad told me last month."

"Another conversation you decided to keep from me?" She ignored the stares from her family members.

"I didn't keep it from you," Clay said, his voice annoyingly reasonable. "I told you more than once to ask your dad."

"You didn't say he was lying to me."

"It wasn't my place. And I'm not sure you'd have believed me if I had. If anything, you'd have packed up and moved out."

True enough, but that didn't temper her mounting anger and resentment.

Suddenly, the room tilted at an odd angle. Dizzy and nauseous, Sierra caught her head as it fell forward.

Clay appeared beside her. "Are you all right?"

"No, I'm not." The world as she knew it was forever changed.

He stroked her hair. "We're going to sort through this."

She almost laughed. Hysterically. He'd said *sort through this* as if they were evaluating a collection of old odds and ends in the garage. "I don't think it's as simple as that."

"Sierra, sweetie," her father implored, "I can see you're upset."

Upset hardly described her current emotional state. She stared at him. His features were the same as always, and, yet, in some ways, they were those of a total stranger's.

Her legs started to tremble. "I have to go."

Clay took her elbow and steadied her.

She pulled away and snapped, "I don't

need your help. Some truthfulness, now *that* I could use."

He stepped back, her hurtful remark hitting the bull's-eye dead center. She stormed off.

Gavin called after her. Ethan, too. She didn't answer.

The other guests had assembled in the kitchen. Sierra hurried past them and out the door. Reaching the sanctuary of the patio, she burst into tears.

So much deception. All of them. Clay, her father, Bud, the Stevensons. And let's not forget herself. Was she any better than her father just because she'd come clean sooner?

Poor Jamie deserved better role models than the ones he had.

What would Dr. Brewster say when she heard about this?

Sierra did laugh then. Bitterly.

"Hey."

She jerked at hearing Clay. "What are you doing here?"

He approached slowly, concern etched on his features. "I hate seeing you distressed."

"Then get back in the house because I'm going to be distressed for a while."

"Come on. Let's take a walk."

"I don't want to walk."

"What about a glass of water?"

"I'm fine."

"What can I do?"

"Check on Jamie for me."

"Is that all?"

She faced him. "Clay, there are just some things you can't control. My entire life going to hell in a handbasket is one of them."

"I'll be waiting inside."

She'd wanted him gone, and she'd got it.

A moment later, she was alone, drifting in what felt like an alternative reality. She hadn't meant to bite Clay's head off. He was trying to be supportive in her time of need.

Why, then, couldn't she turn to him and accept that support?

Because he'd been secretly communicating with Jessica and had had a meeting with her.

And she'd borne Clay's son and gave him up for adoption without telling Clay.

How could the two of them have a secure and happy future with a foundation based on deception?

Leave. Now. The urge came on her again.

She did better on her own, when she could hear her own thoughts, organize her priorities, gain a different perspective.

But where to go?

Removing her cell phone from her pocket, she dialed her attorney Roberto's number, vaguely aware she'd done this before, with disastrous results.

It didn't stop her.

Roberto answered with a brisk "Hello, Sierra."

She didn't miss a beat. "I'm sorry to impose on you, but I don't have anyone else to call."

"What is it?"

"I need a place to stay for a few days. Possibly a week."

Chapter Fourteen

Clay could be patient when the situation called for it. Not today. He was on the verge of exploding.

Sierra had been in the casita for the last hour while he occupied himself in the house and yard with a dozen menial tasks. He'd given her the space she'd asked for, at her family's home and here. But he wasn't going to be shut out indefinitely.

After she'd abandoned the birthday party to sit alone on the back patio and, in his opinion, brood, he'd spoken to her father and brothers. Gavin stayed sore at Clay but did shake his hand eventually. Tensions had remained high, however, and he couldn't wait to leave.

Wayne had significant lost ground to make up, and Clay felt sorry for the man. His first concern, however, was Sierra.

She'd received a momentous blow. But she would recover, and they'd move on. Clay was practical that way.

Crossing the yard, he opened the gate to the casita's small courtyard, remembering the night they'd first made love and he'd jumped the gate in haste. The door was slightly ajar, an indicator that Jamie was napping. Sierra never left the door unlocked if he was awake in case he wandered outside.

Clay knocked and called softly, "Sierra."

She didn't answer. Was she napping, too? Probably. Emotional displays were exhausting. He stood there a moment, debated whether to knock again or return later.

"Come in."

Apparently, she was awake.

He entered quietly so as not to disturb Jamie and came face-to-face with her packing a suitcase.

"What are you doing?"

"I'm leaving for a while, taking Jamie with me. I need some time alone to think."

Leaving? Was she joking? "You can't think here? I won't bother you if that's what concerns you."

She set a pair of folded slacks on top of the already full suitcase and pressed down on the clothes to compress them. "I'd rather get away from everyone and everything. Clear my head. Gain some perspective. Being here reminds me of everything. Confuses me and clouds my judgment."

"And your judgment isn't clouded at your dad's?"

"I'm not staying there."

When she'd originally said she was leaving, Clay had been mad. Now, he was scared. "Where, then?"

She glanced at Jamie sleeping in the crib.

"Sierra. Tell me."

"My attorney's home."

"For how long?"

"Three or four days."

"This is bullshit," he spat out.

"Not so loud, you'll wake up Jamie."

Reining in his frustration, he continued in a lower voice, "You can't just leave."

Her chin jutted out. "You promised me when I moved in that I wasn't chained to you or this place."

"You're not. You can go anytime. But I'm asking you to stay. We can't work on our relationship when we're apart."

"This is about a lot more than our relationship."

"We're in the same boat, Sierra. My dad lied to me, too."

"There's a difference. Your dad's motives were good—to spare his friend embarrassment. My dad's motives were to save himself. I want to forgive him, and I will. I just need time alone and to talk to someone who doesn't have a personal stake in this."

"Good idea. We can see Dr. Brewster together."

She closed the suitcase lid. "Don't take this wrong, but you have a strong personality and strong opinions, and I'm too easily influenced. If I talk to Dr. Brewster, it will be by myself."

"Go easier on your dad. None of us is guiltless when it comes to lying."

"None of us perpetuated a lie for years and years."

She might have, if he hadn't been there for her surprise party the day she arrived home.

His face must have reflected his thoughts

for she zippered the suitcase closed with an angry jerk of her hand.

"Are you punishing me for Jessica?"

"Don't be ridiculous." Her denial was weak at best.

How long until she forgave *him?*

"Okay, stay at your attorney's house for a few days. Just leave Jamie with me."

"What!"

"Jamie's head doesn't need any clearing, and his perspective is fine."

"Absolutely not."

"You've said yourself over and over that he's had too much disruption in his life. I don't think we should put him through any more, especially when it isn't necessary."

"I'm taking him with me."

"We have a joint-custody agreement. I want my five days starting now."

"You can't do that."

"I'm pretty sure I can. If need be, we'll let a judge decide."

Her chest rose and fell rapidly. "You haven't enforced the custody agreement before."

"That's because you were living here." *And we were sleeping together.* "Now, you're leaving."

"I'll be gone a week at the most."

"No problem. I can watch Jamie for a week."

"Don't do this, Clay."

"I'm asking you the same thing."

"I can't stay here," she said in a thready whisper.

"Why?"

"It's too confining. Too crowded."

No more confining or crowded than her attorney's home. "That's what you do, isn't it? When things get tough, you run for the hills."

"I do not!"

"Oh, come on. You turned down a full-ride scholarship and instead went to college in another state right after your mom died and the ranch started to fail. You cut off your family and me when you found out you were pregnant. You left your old job and your friends in California to come here because you couldn't handle your anxieties and being a single mother. And now you're slinking off to your attorney's house after a fight with your dad."

"It was more than a fight."

"Grow up, Sierra. Start facing your problems instead of avoiding them."

"How dare you criticize me!" Anger flashed in those wide eyes. "I may not cope well with my problems but at least I'm not a control freak."

"This isn't a matter of me trying to control you. It's you taking my son from me. *Again!* If clearing your head and getting perspective is really your goal, you can do that without Jamie."

"You know I can't be separated from him."

"You should have thought of that before deciding to leave."

"I'm not the bad person here. My dad is."

"Don't go, Sierra. When has leaving ever worked out for you?"

"When has pushing people into doing what you want ever worked out for you? Is that why Jessica left?"

Clay recoiled as if stabbed with an iron poker.

Was Sierra right? Had he pushed Jessica into having children when she wasn't ready? Put his own desire to start a family ahead of hers for a career?

"What about your job? You leaving that, too?"

"I'm sorry to put you in a spot."

"We have an employment contract."

"That allows for sick time."

"You're not sick."

"Whatever." She grabbed a tissue from the box on the nightstand and dabbed her nose. "Short my pay."

"The wild-horse auction is next weekend. Everyone is counting on you."

"All the files are in order, and I left detailed notes on the desk. A temp can handle the rest."

"Is there nothing you care about more than yourself?"

"Is there *anything* you care about *besides* yourself?" she shot back.

"You. My son. Our dads. Patching up this god-awful mess and putting our families back on track. I'm not sure how to accomplish that, but I damn well know the answer isn't running off to my attorney's."

She set the suitcase on the floor. "You pegged me earlier. I fold under pressure. And whether you intend it or not, you pressure me. I'm not the kind of person who stands up for herself well."

"You're standing up to me."

"Are you really going to fight me for Jamie?"

"If you walk out that door, I most certainly am."

"What if I don't go to my attorney's? What if I stay at my dad's instead?"

"I thought you said you couldn't go there, either."

"I'm thinking you're right. I should face my dad. Deal with his lie."

"Then by all means, go." He was through pleading with her. "But leave Jamie here."

"You can visit him every day at the ranch."

For someone so adamant about not seeing her dad a minute ago, she was making a pretty quick turnaround.

"Do you really need space or do you simply want to get away from me?"

She closed her eyes. "I don't know anymore."

Nothing she'd said until now hurt worse than that. "We have a custody agreement, and we're going to stick to it."

"It feels like you're the one punishing me." She pressed a hand to her chest, rubbed it as if her heart ached. "Why don't you just admit it? You don't trust me."

"Should I? You did hide my son from me."

"And you've hidden things from me, too. Pretty recently, in fact."

"I told you, I was trying to avoid an argument."

"Well, big surprise. We're arguing."

Clay lost his temper, aware he was exhibiting the very stereotypical control-freak trait she'd accused him of. "I've bent over backward for you. The casita. The job. Letting you take Jamie with you to the office. The counseling sessions. I've given a hundred and ten percent."

"I've given, too. I agreed to move in with you for Jamie's sake and our relationship. And I've been a damn good employee."

"Good employees don't quit with no notice."

"I'll be back."

"Permanently or to pick up Jamie?"

"That's not fair."

Clay expelled a harsh breath. "I can't live every day wondering if you'll disappear because my preference to eat dinner at six is too controlling."

"I'm not that extreme."

"I've been committed to you and Jamie since the day you returned. I wish you could say the same."

"A short breather to reevaluate and take stock of the situation isn't a lack of commitment."

Jamie woke up and started to cry. Incredibly, he'd slept through the entire argument.

Sierra and Clay started toward him and

bottlenecked at the foot of the crib. They stared at each other in stormy silence for several seconds, neither giving an inch.

Finally, Clay let her pass. Apparently his dad did raise him to be a gentleman.

Sierra lifted Jamie into her arms. The second he saw Clay, he reached for him, his face puffy and mottled from sleep.

"Hey, there, pal."

"Da, da, da, da."

Sierra's features caved, her pain striking him square in the gut.

In one afternoon she'd had her entire belief system felled. That would send even the strongest individual retreating to lick their wounds. He was about to tell her to take Jamie with her when she abruptly handed him to Clay.

"All this fighting is getting us nowhere."

He went weak with relief. She'd changed her mind. They were going to solve their problems and everything would go back to the way it was.

"I agree," he said. "Let's not talk anymore tonight. We'll have some dinner, take Jamie on a walk."

"You can. I won't be here." She went to the bed and grabbed her suitcase. "We'll start with two days, then go to five. I'll see you

Monday evening when I pick up Jamie. Or you can drop him off at Dad's, whichever's more convenient for you."

Clay held Jamie close, like a shield, words escaping him.

Of all the times for her to spontaneously overcome her separation anxieties.

"I love you, honey bun." She gave Jamie a desperate hug and kiss on the cheek. Then, looking straight ahead, marched out the door, the only sign of her distress a slight wobble in her gait.

She was either the bravest person Clay knew or the biggest coward.

What about him?

Right this moment, he was alone.

"Ma, ma, ma." Jamie poked Clay on the side of the head.

He could imagine his son saying, "Hey, idiot. You just let the woman we love leave."

And he'd be right.

The wild-horse auction was starting in— Sierra glanced at her watch—two hours.

Unable to completely walk away from the job, she'd handled several last-minute tasks from home—her father's home—and spoken daily on the phone with the temp Clay had hired. It wasn't the same.

She could see the auction unfolding in her mind's eye.

The ranch hands grooming and exercising the mustangs under her brothers' careful supervision so they would look their best and behave well. The foreman and his crew grading the dirt and insuring the arena was in tip-top condition, the bleachers swept, the pens tidy and the grounds spotless.

Any minute, the auctioneer and his assistant would arrive and set up in the announcer's booth. Dallas was probably arranging her photographer's table and inventorying her supplies. The media would arrive soon. One local TV station had agreed to send a reporter and camera operator and a small local paper had promised coverage.

The only individual not showing up was the head cashier.

Her.

Sierra had recruited Sage to take over rather than simply assist, as was the original plan. Cashiering wasn't complicated, and there were the notes Sierra had left. Sage would have no trouble.

Sierra moped. She was a good employee,

not the kind who abandoned ship in the middle of a big event.

Yet she'd done exactly that. Left her job, her son and Clay.

Talk about selfish.

She missed them. All of them. Clay, too.

Those last weeks together were the happiest she'd had since their affair. If only he'd given her those few days she needed to think, trusted her enough not to take off with Jamie, she'd be with him now.

No sooner had she shown up on her father's doorstep a week ago than the two of them had talked. Unresolved issues remained, but they were making headway. With Gavin and Ethan as well. Not that Ethan had been upset with her. Gavin—that was a different story. He was disappointed she wasn't working the auction. After several awkward meals, they'd cleared the air enough to eat companionably if not noisily and rowdily like before.

Sierra hadn't realized how similar she and her father were—they both tended to avoid their problems. Where they differed was that she ran while her father shut down completely.

Checking her watch again, she sighed. She should be at the auction.

After all the hurt she'd caused her family,

all the assistance they'd given her, she owed them not to bail at the last hour. In this valley, mustangs were synonymous with the Powell name and the plight of wild horses was close to their hearts, a vital part of their personal history to pass down to their children and grandchildren. To Jamie.

It was also a cause important to Clay.

He had Jamie, would for another four days as per their parenting schedule.

She hadn't forgotten about her son. Heaven forbid. But she didn't obsess about him when he wasn't with her. Not anymore. The breakup with Clay—she'd stopped kidding herself and calling it "time away"—had had one positive impact on her. She'd mostly gotten over her separation anxiety. There were moments, but then she'd remind herself Clay was a good father and wouldn't let anything happen to Jamie.

She wished he'd taken the same tender care of her love for him.

Sierra didn't regret her decision. It really was for the best, as she kept telling herself. Clay must agree. He didn't act as though he wanted a reconciliation when they met to hand over Jamie.

God, that sounded awful. Their son wasn't

a borrowed tool to be exchanged when the other person was done using it.

She wondered if Clay had Jamie with him at the auction or if he'd hired Cassie to babysit. No, her niece would be with her fellow equestrian drill team members selling refreshments at the concession stand.

Did the drill team need more ice? Sierra could buy some and take it over. She'd be welcomed.

What message would that send Clay? She'd been wrong? She was sorry? She wanted to try again? She wasn't a quitter and finished the jobs she started?

Apparently she was less dedicated to relationships than jobs.

She'd been so scared after seeing Jessica in the diner and discovering Clay had met with her, terrified when her father's duplicity was revealed. It was too much like looking at her own reflection.

Sierra had once viewed honesty as fluid, able to change shape depending on the individual's needs.

It was an excuse she'd used to justify her own actions.

The last few weeks had taught her much. What to do with her new education?

She tackled the laundry in an attempt to stop dwelling on the auction and Clay. In her bedroom—the bedroom that would belong to Gavin and Sage's baby once he or she was born—she grabbed the laundry bag.

Finding a new place to live and a new job were a priority, but she'd been dragging her feet, even turning down a second, in-person, interview with the company that had called. When she'd mentioned her lack of motivation to Dr. Brewster, the counselor had turned the tables on Sierra by posing questions like "Why do you think you're procrastinating?" and "How do you feel about quitting your job?"

Miserable, all right? I feel miserable.

Sierra took her frustration out on the dirty clothes, ruthlessly stuffing them into the washing machine. As she was making a second trip to the laundry room with some of the girls' clothes, the doorbell rang.

She glimpsed through the peephole but didn't recognize the caller, whose face was averted as she dug through her purse. It must be one of the ranch customers with a problem. Sierra opened the door.

"Hello, can I—" Her vocal chords froze.

"Hi, Sierra. I'm glad you're here. I hope

you don't mind me showing up without calling first."

Oh, yes, she minded.

"I wasn't sure you'd see me."

No fooling.

"Can I come in? I promise to take no more than a minute. I'm leaving for Texas tomorrow and wanted to talk to you."

Convinced she was making a giant mistake, Sierra stepped aside to let Jessica enter.

Chapter Fifteen

"Care to sit?" Sierra indicated the living room with a flimsy wave of her hand. Had she really just invited Clay's ex-wife into the house?

Jessica's gaze swept the interior as she followed Sierra. "I'd forgotten how charming and homey this place is."

"It's been a while, I suppose."

"Years."

Jessica had visited the Powells on occasion when she and Clay were dating.

"I'm sorry about your divorce." Good grief. Could Sierra have made a stupider remark? Her brain must have disconnected from her mouth.

"Thank you." Jessica sat on the sofa, brushed her stylishly messy bangs from her face and smoothed her wrinkle-free pants.

"What do you want to talk about?" Her initial surprise having passed, Sierra was curious, though she remained cautious.

"I came to apologize."

"What for?" Her stomach tightened. Something more had happened at Jessica's recent meeting with Clay.

Were his denials nothing but more lies?

"Stealing Clay away from you. Your life, his, and that of your son, would be vastly different if I'd been less jealous and able to admit Clay wasn't the man for me."

"I'm confused. Are you referring to two years ago?"

Jessica nodded. "I'd heard you and he were seeing each other. Mustang Valley is a small community. I didn't want Clay for myself, but I didn't want anyone else to have him. Not so soon. Not before I'd found a new man." She smiled sadly. "I wasn't the best person in those days. Marriage, failing at it and surviving divorce changed me. Oh, gosh." She looked chagrined. "Did I just utter a cliché?"

Jessica had changed. Goodie for her. As far as Sierra was concerned, one I-came-to-apologize speech didn't make everything okay. Jessica's fickle whims had wreaked chaos on too many lives. "Isn't it a little late for this?"

"Possibly. Possibly not. I heard you had moved out of Clay's casita."

"He told you?" Sierra's twisted stomach turned inside out. He was still communicating with Jessica despite his promise.

"I haven't seen or spoken to Clay since we met at the coffee shop and I signed the insurance form."

"Then how—"

"I saw Caitlin at the clinic yesterday. My godmother's blood-sugar level dropped, and I rushed her in for a quick check. Caitlin mentioned you. Actually, I asked how you and Clay were, and she reluctantly told me."

"Oh." Sierra had jumped to conclusions.

"You know, Clay always wanted children, and he adores Jamie."

"Yes, he does."

"He loves you, too."

Sierra must have misheard. "I beg your pardon?"

"I think he fell in love with you two years ago, he just didn't realize it. He and I had dated a long, long time. Old habits are hard to break." She stood, smoothed her pants again.

Caitlin now recognized the gesture as a nervous one. "Don't let him get away again."

The last person in the world Sierra thought she should take advice from was Jessica.

Except the advice was pretty darn good.

She left, and Sierra shut the door behind her, slumping against it. Clay loved her! At least according to Jessica he did.

Sierra had been a fool, and not for the first time. She'd permitted her fear of rejection to color her judgment, manufactured reasons to reject Clay before he rejected her.

How to tell him she loved and trusted him in a way he couldn't possibly misunderstand or misinterpret?

Easy. She'd go to the auction. Where she should have been all morning.

Changing her clothes, she dashed outside to her SUV. The minute she hit the end of the driveway, she pulled her cell phone from her purse. The first call she made was to her father, the second one to Blythe. They were both at the auction. Sierra's request, the same to each of them, was readily and excitedly granted.

Parking at Clay's house, she half walked, half jogged the short distance to the arena. The place was already packed, the bleachers full. She searched frantically for Clay and Jamie, responding with a distracted "Hi, have you seen Clay?" when people greeted her. She finally spotted him near the announcer's stand, being interviewed by the TV reporter. A moment later he noticed her and briefly lost his train of thought before continuing.

She stood to the side and waited until the interview was concluded. The reporter thanked Clay and left with the camera operator to film more footage. Sierra approached slowly.

"If you're looking for Jamie, he's with my mother."

"I know. I didn't come here to see Jamie." She longed to throw herself at him, but his wary expression held her at bay.

"Then why?"

"I've been stupid lately. About work and… other things."

"What other things?" His control cracked a tiny fraction.

She intended to split it wide open. "Give me my job back and I'll tell you."

"That mare and colt are the best of the bunch," Ethan observed. "They should bring in decent money."

Clay stood at the far end of the arena fence, half listening to his friend, his attention all over the place. He couldn't take his mind off Sierra.

She'd come back for her job.

Not him.

She'd barely made her cryptic remark about "other things" when Clay was called away to resolve a problem. With a "We'll chat later," she'd hurried to meet with the auctioneer and his assistant. Clay had glimpsed her a short time later scurrying across the open area to the office in the barn.

He'd wanted to talk then, not later, but the auction had started and was quickly in full swing. As cashier, Sierra would be busy processing paperwork and accepting funds for an hour or two after the auction closed.

Could he wait?

"I'm glad the other horses were adopted, I just wish they'd brought higher prices," Ethan continued, unaware of Clay's turmoil. "Unless that grant money comes through, the sanctuary will go broke in a few months."

"We'll think of something," Clay muttered distractedly.

"Hey! What's up?" Ethan elbowed Clay in the ribs. "Sierra tying you in knots again?"

"I'm concentrating on the auction."

"It's like that, you know."

He glanced over his shoulder at the office in the distance. Sierra hadn't emerged since going inside. "What is?"

"When you're in love." Ethan shook his head as if accepting a dismal truth.

"I'm not in love."

"Yeah. Sure. And the sky is green."

Was he in love with Sierra? Clay gave his head a dismal shake mimicking Ethan's.

He was sunk. In love with a woman who didn't love him.

But she had come back. Asked for her old job. Mentioned being stupid about "other things."

"I need to find your sister."

"Wait." Ethan grabbed Clay's jacket sleeve and restrained him. "The bidding is starting on the mare and colt."

They watched as the last two horses up for auction were led into the arena. The auctioneer recounted their history to the audience, when, where and how they'd been rounded up and what training they'd been given. Then he talked up the duo's good qualities, emphasizing their potential as all-around Western pleasure mounts.

"Okee dokie, ladies and gents." His voice rang out from the speakers. "What do you say we open up the bidding at two hundred dollars for the pair."

At first, no one raised their hand. When the price dropped to twenty-five dollars, the bidding took off and didn't stop. The wranglers kept the mare and colt calm while the ring men stationed themselves in front of the bleachers and alerted the auctioneer with a loud whoop when a bid was made.

Before Clay realized it, the price was up to a thousand. Then, two thousand. Twenty-five hundred. Three thousand.

What the heck?

He scanned the audience, trying to determine who was bidding so furiously on the horses. He didn't recognize either of the men, one an old-timer and the other a businessman in a suit and tie.

"Twenty thousand dollars." The call came from the businessman.

The audience fell silent for several shocked seconds, then broke out into hoots and hollers.

"I have twenty thousand dollars," the auctioneer shouted, disbelief in his voice. "Do I have twenty-one thousand?"

"Dang!" The old-timer threw up his arms in defeat. "I'd have to rob a bank."

"Going once, going twice, sold to number…" He waited for the buyer to hold up his card. "Eighty-six."

"Hot damn." Ethan grabbed Clay's arm and jostled it, grinning ridiculously. "That's enough money to run the sanctuary for a year, maybe two."

"Who is that guy?"

"Let's find out. Looks like that TV reporter is about to interview him."

They made their way across the open area to the crowd that had formed around the businessman and the reporter. Sierra waited on the other side. He'd have gone to her but then noticed a man standing beside her. Before he could manage a closer look, someone stepped in front of him and blocked his view.

"Wow," the TV reporter gushed as the camera operator filmed and Dallas snapped pictures, "that was some purchase. Tell us about yourself and your plans for the horses?"

"I didn't buy them for myself. I'm a broker with MRB Trade and Commerce, acting on behalf of my client. He's the one who purchased the horses."

"Can you give us his name?"

"Certainly. He's here, in fact." The broker inclined his head. "Mr. Bud Duvall."

"Your dad?" Ethan exclaimed in a booming voice. "He bought the horses?"

Clay's thoughts exactly. "Excuse me." He wedged between two people in an attempt to get closer, Ethan behind him.

His dad stepped up to the reporter, taking the place of his banker. Sierra, holding Jamie, and Wayne were with him.

What in the world was going on?

Finally, when Clay's patience was about to snap, he and Ethan broke free of the crowd.

The rest of Ethan's family surrounded Clay's father. Gavin, Sage, Caitlin and the girls. Clay's mother was also there.

He went to her. "Mom?"

She took his hand and patted it, then told him, "Shh, your father's talking."

"People who've lived in these parts a long time know that the Duvalls and Powells were once close as kin." Clay's dad nervously wiped his sweaty brow with his handkerchief. "Unfortunately, we had a bit of a falling-out, I guess you'd say. Spent a lot of years being needlessly mad at each other. It took this little guy here to bring us to our senses." He ruffled Jamie's hair. "And this here gal." He squeezed Sierra's shoulder.

Clay watched, stunned.

"I'd like to present this check, twenty thousand for the purchase of the horses and an additional twenty thousand dollars for the Powell Wild Mustang Sanctuary."

A gasp erupted from the crowd.

"I make this donation in memory of Louise Powell." He handed the check to Sierra. "Late wife of my friend Wayne. It can't change what happened, but maybe it, and this boy, will give us a second chance."

Wayne extended his hand to Clay's father, visibly moved. "I can't thank you enough. For *everything*."

"Water under the bridge, pal. Water under the bridge." Clay's dad pulled Wayne into a warm bear hug.

The rest of the families converged on them. There were more hugs and tears. Everyone stood back a moment while Gavin and Clay's dad exchanged words and shook hands.

Clay didn't join his family—his *two* families. He made straight for Sierra and Jamie.

"You knew about the donation," he said.

"Not until right before the auction started. Your dad met me in the office."

"He's always liked being the center of attention." Clay chuckled. "In this case, I approve."

"I was thinking." She jiggled Jamie, who'd started to fuss.

"About *other things*?"

"Yes. If our dads are able to put the past behind them, maybe we can—"

Clay cut her off with a kiss. Then another and another until Jamie protested noisily at being squished between them.

"There's something I've been meaning to tell you," he said. "Something I should have told you weeks ago."

"What?"

"I love you." He lost himself in her startling blue eyes. "And I want to marry you. Not just because of Jamie, but because I can't live without you one more day. I know I'm being pushy."

"You're not." She looped an arm around his neck. "I love you, too."

"Let's start over. Take it one day at a time. You can move back into the casita, if you're comfortable with that, or stay at your dad's."

"I'd rather live in the house with you."

"Okay. On two conditions."

"More legal agreements?" She smiled coyly.

"Not exactly. First, you accept my proposal."

She captured Jamie's chin and turned his face toward hers. "I'm not sure. What do you think, honey bun? Should I marry your daddy?"

Jamie squealed and babbled, "Da, da, da, be."

"I think that's a yes. What's the second condition?"

Clay struggled to get a grip on his soaring emotions. "We tear up that employment contract. I don't want you working for me."

"No?"

"I want you to be my partner in the rodeo arena."

"Seriously?" Her eyes glittered with excitement. "Because I'd be good at that, and I'd—"

He kissed her again, and it was the sweetest one yet.

"I called your mom and my dad on the way here," she admitted, reluctantly extracting herself from his embrace. "They've agreed to share babysitting duties. As much as I love having Jamie in the office with me, it's too hard to get my work done and take care of him, too."

"Are you ready for that?"

She gazed lovingly at him. "I'm ready for anything, cowboy."

Clay reached for her.

"Hey, you three," Ethan hollered, "break it up. We're in public."

"I'll kiss my fiancée in public or anywhere I want," Clay answered without looking away from Sierra.

"Fiancée!" Blythe charged them, the rest of the Powells hot on her heels. "I'm so happy for you. I've been hoping and praying you two would get married."

"Wait!" Dallas called, her camera in hand. "We have to take photos. Everyone, squeeze together." She snapped away. "Now, one of Clay, Sierra and Jamie."

"Can we get an extra copy?" Clay asked, already intending to display the picture with the others in his office.

"You bet!"

"How you holding up?" he asked Sierra when the commotion started to die down.

"I'm great. Happy." She kissed Jamie's cheek, then Clay's. "I can't believe it. Last January, I was alone. Cut off from my family, turning my back on my friends, losing my job and my apartment. And now…this. Jamie. You. Our families reunited. I have to be the luckiest person alive."

"We could get luckier." Clay arched a brow at her. "Have another kid or two. If that's not too controlling."

"Maybe a younger sister for Jamie." She

smiled coyly, and Clay fell deeper in love. "But I have my own condition."

"Name it."

"We get married first."

"You free next weekend?" he joked.

She called his bluff and rocked his world by answering with a resounding "Yes!"

* * * * *

Get 2 Free Books,
Plus 2 Free Gifts —
just for trying the Reader Service!

Get 2 Free Books,
Plus 2 Free Gifts —
just for trying the Reader Service!

Get 2 Free Books,

Plus 2 Free Gifts— just for trying the Reader Service!

Get 2 Free Books,
Plus 2 Free Gifts—
just for trying the Reader Service!

Get 2 Free Books,
Plus 2 Free Gifts –
just for trying the Reader Service!

STRS17

Get 2 Free Books,

Plus 2 Free Gifts—
just for trying the Reader Service!

READERSERVICE.COM

Manage your account online!

- Review your order history
- Manage your payments
- Update your address

> *We've designed the*
> *Reader Service website*
> *just for you.*

Enjoy all the features!

- Discover new series available to you, and read excerpts from any series.
- Respond to mailings and special monthly offers.
- Browse the Bonus Bucks catalog and online-only exculsives.
- Share your feedback.

Visit us at:
ReaderService.com